MISSING

MASON BLACK (BOOK 1)

ADAM NICHOLLS

Copyright © 2018 by Adam Nicholls
All rights reserved. No part of this publication may be reproduced, distributed, or transmitted in any form or by any means, including photocopying, recording, or other electronic or mechanical methods, without the prior written permission of the publisher, except in the case of brief quotations embodied in critical reviews and certain other non-commercial uses permitted by copyright law. For permission requests, write to the publisher, addressed "Attention: Permissions Coordinator," at the address below.

contact@adamnichollsauthor.com

CONTENTS

MISSING

Chapter 1	3
Chapter 2	6
Chapter 3	9
Chapter 4	12
Chapter 5	14
Chapter 6	17
Chapter 7	20
Chapter 8	23
Chapter 9	26
Chapter 10	30
Chapter 11	33
Chapter 12	36
Chapter 13	40
Chapter 14	43
Chapter 15	46
Chapter 16	50
Chapter 17	53
Chapter 18	56
Chapter 19	59
Chapter 20	62
Chapter 21	68
Chapter 22	71
Chapter 23	73
Chapter 24	75
Chapter 25	77
Chapter 26	79
Chapter 27	82

Chapter 28	87
Chapter 29	91
Chapter 30	95
Chapter 31	98
Chapter 32	102
Chapter 33	106
Chapter 34	109
Chapter 35	112
Chapter 36	114
Chapter 37	118
Chapter 38	121
Chapter 39	125
Chapter 40	128
Chapter 41	131
Chapter 42	135
Chapter 43	138
Chapter 44	143
Chapter 45	147
Chapter 46	150
Chapter 47	153
Chapter 48	157
Chapter 49	163
Chapter 50	167
Chapter 51	170
Chapter 52	174
Chapter 53	177
Chapter 54	180
Chapter 55	183
Chapter 56	187
Chapter 57	190
Chapter 58	192
Chapter 59	195
Chapter 60	198
Chapter 61	200
Chapter 62	203

Chapter 63	207
Chapter 64	211
Chapter 65	214
Chapter 66	217
Chapter 67	220
Chapter 68	223
Chapter 69	225
Chapter 70	228
Chapter 71	230
Chapter 72	233
Chapter 73	236
Chapter 74	239
Chapter 75	242
Chapter 76	246
Chapter 77	248
Chapter 78	250
Chapter 79	253
Chapter 80	256
Chapter 81	259
Chapter 82	262
Chapter 83	265
Chapter 84	268
Chapter 85	270
Chapter 86	272
Chapter 87	275
Chapter 88	278
Chapter 89	282
Chapter 90	285
Also by	287
Afterword	289
About the Author	291

For Charlotte.
Always.

MISSING

CHAPTER ONE

Little Missy Daniels stumbled through the dark woods, the killer chasing close behind.

While trying not to think about the things he'd done to her, she spent the last of her depleted energy desperately picking up her pace. Uncaring branches snapped at her bare legs, and sharp twigs crunched painfully underfoot. Her frightened panting escalated.

"I'm going to get you!" the man bellowed, thick anger resonating in his booming voice. "You're mine, Missy!"

But Missy didn't want to believe it. For days he'd kept her imprisoned, locking her in the corner of that dark room with no food or water, only acknowledging her existence to threaten her with whatever new surgical tool he'd procured. The fear of those horrendous tools drove her to run faster, faster... until she tripped.

Missy fell flat, planting her face in the rotting mulch leaves of the forest, their sickly sweet stench making her gag. At only eight years old, barely able to take care of herself, she didn't believe she could make it out of there alive. Yet, she'd outrun him this far…

"I hear you, little girl!" he screamed after her, his voice menacing.

Up you get, she told herself. *Mommy is waiting for you to come home.*

Shoving her palms deep into the oozing mud, she pushed herself up and half crawled, half dragged herself to a nearby bush, praying its darkness would conceal her. Hidden amongst the dense thicket, tiny thorns stabbing at her soft skin, she waited, slowly expelling desperate breaths into cupped hands in an effort to keep silent.

Through the downpour, she could hear him slipping and sliding in the filth, and for a moment she thought he might actually walk on by without noticing her. But then he stopped suddenly, his looming figure standing just a few feet from her dark hiding place.

Missy felt her pulse quicken and her stomach muscles tense. Her breaths became raspy, more rapid, while a high-pitched whine crept through her pursed lips. She pulled her little hands closer, silencing herself as best she could.

But it was too late.

The man stepped toward her, glancing over his shoulder as if about to reveal a big secret. Had he seen her? If he hadn't, he surely would soon.

Missy clutched herself tighter, shivering in the wet undergrowth. She'd never really believed in God—she was too young for such nonsense—but was now silently praying that, if she made it out of there alive, she would—

The hand rocketed toward her, groping at her torn dress.

"Get over here," the man spat, dragging her out of the tangled bush with a strong, unyielding hand, angrier now than he had ever been.

Desperate to break free, Missy kicked and screamed, struggling in vain as mud and leaves shot out from under her flailing feet. But it was no use. No matter what she did, she couldn't escape his deadly clutches.

She had tried to run, had failed, and was now being dragged toward her inevitable gruesome end.

CHAPTER TWO

"I want a divorce."

It was that simple, four words that could bring the strongest of men to their knees. Mason *wanted* to drop to his knees, his heart plummeting, but pride wouldn't allow it. Instead, he recovered from his shock, took a big, dry swallow and said, "Okay."

"Okay? *Okay?*" Sandra screamed at him, clattering dishes into the kitchen sink. "You're not even asking why?"

Mason could hardly believe it and desperately searched for an explanation. "You think I work too much. You... you honestly believe I don't care about you? Look at the room you're in. My work paid for this. For all this!" he added, waving his arms around to make his point. "Without my work, we wouldn't be able to have the family and lifestyle we have."

"Give it up, Mason. You're not even a real cop." Although Sandra's eyes usually shone with an inquisitive light, now there was only regret as she mumbled those words.

It stung for Mason, too. After all, he *had* given up his work as a detective so he could spend more time with the family. After he'd set up a casual business as a private investigator, he could sense the family becoming much happier. Perhaps that was why it shook him so much to suddenly learn of his wife's unhappiness.

"I'm sorry," she said. "But I'm just not happy. I want you to leave."

"Leave? Sandra, this is my house, too."

"Please, just give us some space."

Mason stood, his expression blank as he tried to figure out where this bombshell had come from. Left field didn't do it justice. His eyes subconsciously drifted to the dining table, coming to rest on a half-empty bottle of wine. *That's not enough to get her drunk*, he thought, dismissing the notion her outburst was driven by inebriation.

"Fine. I'll take a couple days. We'll talk in the morning." He was halfway out the door when she caught up to him, snapping at his heels like an aggressive dog.

"No, Mason. I want you out, gone. I want a divorce. Are you hearing me? D-i-v-o-r—"

"What exactly is wrong with you, huh?" Mason stopped and turned. "Why can't we just work things out like we usually do? That's how it works. You tell me what's wrong and I fix it, then you realize it's not enough and the cycle starts again. Why can't we just go back to that?"

For once, Sandra was quiet, assessing him in silence.

"No. It wasn't making me happy. Just go. Wait until I call you. Understood?"

Mason grabbed furiously for his coat, missing it, which enraged him even more. "Fine. Fine!" he barked, though he wasn't. "I want to say goodbye to Amy." He pictured the hurt on his daughter's face if she'd been here to witness this drama. Thankfully, she was in her room, chilling out with music like most thirteen-year-olds.

"No. Not now." Sandra edged him toward the door, her face impassive. "Just go and wait. Like I said."

Mason was about to protest when the cell phone in his pocket jingled. A quick glance told him it was Evelyn, his sister and best friend, though every bit his opposite. If it were anybody else he might have ignored it, but Evie was more than his sister—she was his news correspondent.

"I'll come by tomorrow," he said to Sandra and headed out the door, unintentionally proving her point. Steeling himself to head into the downpour, he strode to his car and knew she was shaking her head behind him.

"Don't bother." The door slammed before the words had even left her lips.

Hustling into the driver's seat, Mason took the call. "Hey, Evie."

"Hey. Are you busy?" The urgency in her voice demanded attention.

"What is it?"

"It's Missy Daniels; they've found her body."

CHAPTER THREE

Mason pulled up to the beachfront parking lot and immediately saw the commotion. An officer recognized his car and waved him through. He parked, squeezed his way through the nosey crowd, and soon arrived at the police cordon.

"Well, you have a face like thunder." Evie stopped him, a concerned look behind her thick black-rimmed glasses. She looked exactly like the intellectual she was. The fancy camera in her hand suggested she was press, but in reality she was more like an independent blogger, famous for publishing a hasty report revealing the shady shenanigans of a government agency the previous year. Entrepreneurship ran in the family.

"It's a long story," Mason told her, keen to focus on the task at hand. "Have you seen Bill?"

"Yep. This way."

Evie raised the yellow police tape and he ducked under. Approached by a police officer, Mason flashed his

PI badge and flicked up the collar of his trench coat before walking on. The chilled rain was heavy enough to soak through, but it was the least of his worries.

"Mason," said Detective Bill Harvey, who shook his hand with a firm grip. "Thanks for coming."

It comforted Mason to know his ex-partner was still a close friend. Ever since leaving the force, Bill had remained a solid and reliable part of his life.

"I'll give you boys a minute," Evie said before disappearing into the crowd.

"It's a confirmed match, Mason. Missy Daniels. Apparently you were working the case?"

"I was." Mason paused and shook his head. "I am." He looked down at the body and felt immediate sadness. "What happened here?"

"Strangled to death. We believe the body was moved here afterward." Bill knelt and pointed at the deep lacerations. "These cuts were made prior to death, we think."

The scene before him was a bloody mess. The girl was naked, her body spread into the shape of a grisly star. The pinky finger of her left hand had been removed, either with expert surgical precision or one swift swipe of a hefty blade. Her tormented eyes were wide with fear, and her skin was already pale. Leaning in, Mason thought she'd begun to smell, but hoped it was his imagination. Most concerning of all, however, was the message.

"None for the dame?" Mason asked, reading the arranged pile of rocks by the girl's feet.

"That's why I called you, buddy. We think it's *him*."

Mason felt his heart skip a beat, his face flushing with

rage and panic despite the coolness of the rain. "I thought he'd stopped. I hoped—"

"I know, but it matches the pattern," Bill interjected. "Look, this is 'Baa, Baa, Black Sheep,' right? I was thinking it might be because the girl is black?" But as a detective of the San Francisco Police Department, he should have been smart enough to know better.

"No. It's just a stupid lullaby. His own twisted way of showing off." Mason turned and stalked away, shielding his eyes against the harsh flashing red/blue of the parked cruiser lights.

"Where are you going?" Bill called after him.

Mason stopped. "I took the case. I want to tell the girl's mother before she sees it on the news."

Bill simply nodded as a cruel gust of wind swept across the ocean and blasted rain at them in a furious wave.

Drenched, freezing, and disturbed, Mason headed back to his Mustang, where Evie stood with her back pressed to the door.

"Get off." Mason waved a hand. "What do you think you're doing?"

"What does it look like? I'm coming with you." She removed her rain-speckled glasses, the usual signal that she was ready for action. "I need a ride home."

Mason sighed, too drained to argue. "Get in. I need to make a stop on the way."

"Sure," Evie said. "Whatever it takes to spend time with my brother."

If only she'd known what was really happening.

CHAPTER FOUR

Look at these morons. They're nothing but sheep.

The Lullaby Killer stood among the crowd, but he wasn't one of them. The appalling way they pushed and shoved at each other to get a glimpse of the body only repulsed him.

How sick can a person be, eager to share the news they'd seen a dead girl? Do they want to show off to their peers? Feel as though they've been let in on a secret? It's fucking lunacy.

But he'd seen it first, and nobody could take that away from him.

A small gap in the crowd opened up, enough to view his own masterpiece. He couldn't deny it; leaving a message in the rocks was a nice touch. It was just sufficient to make it look like a signature, but not enough to lead them to him. There was no real meaning to it, only the first thing that had come to his mind: sheep.

And everyone would pity the poor victim, bright and

beautiful young Missy Daniels. *Oh, but she wasn't poor.* Truth was, there'd been nothing poor about her. She was smart and pretty, and everyone loved her. Top of her class. A real bitch.

Dislodging him from his moment of pride, the killer saw something he hadn't seen in years: the black Shelby Mustang parked to the side of the road. The detective climbed out, and his blood thickened as he watched him stroll toward the scene, ready to tackle crime once again.

I thought he'd retired from the police force?

Considering how close Mr. Black had come to catching him all those years ago, the Lullaby Killer knew he'd have to be more careful. Any move he was yet to make would be inspected by the detective, and the Lullaby Killer would not let anything—or anyone—stop him now.

Determined to seek shelter from the rain, the killer edged away from the crowd. What else could he do tonight, other than go on the prowl for his next victim? It would be the perfect distraction for him, that euphoric sensation of power as he made them scream and beg for mercy.

Why can't these people see I'm helping them? Isn't it obvious I only target the douchebags, the privileged, and the kids with spoilt upbringings? I'm improving the next generation, too. They bring it on themselves.

Still, he would have plenty of time to show them, to make them understand.

The killer headed back to his vehicle, started the engine, and began his search.

CHAPTER FIVE

Evie—as small as her brother was big—reclined in the passenger seat. If Mason knew her as well as he thought he did, she was fighting a strong urge to put her feet up on the dashboard. She was learning, at last, and that was good.

"Where are we going?" she asked, sensing something was wrong.

"I have to swing by Missy's house. Somebody needs to tell her parents."

"Sure, but it doesn't have to be you."

Mason said nothing.

"So... you think it's him? Is he back?"

"I don't know," he said, eyes fixed on the road. "Could be."

"You don't suspect a copycat?" Evie persisted.

"No."

"Why not?"

"I just don't." Mason huffed loud enough to make the hint, but it failed to land.

"Come on, you must have some—"

"Listen," he snapped, "I don't know any more than you at this point. I have enough on my mind without worrying about leaking details to the press."

"*The press*? Is that all I am to you? Jeez, thanks a lot."

They sat in silence for the rest of the journey, the car speeding through the deluge. When they arrived, Mason took a deep breath, climbed out of the Mustang, and prepared himself.

"Sorry," Evie mumbled, but Mason shut the door. If she wanted to apologize, he'd rather she did it when he didn't have his back turned.

Shaking off his uneasy mood, Mason climbed the few steps to the house, an upmarket place and surprisingly nice for an unemployed single mother. He rapped on the door, unsure exactly how to phrase what he had to say.

The door swung open, and a tired-looking black woman stood there staring at him. She must have sensed something was wrong, as she didn't say a word. Shaking, she retreated into her house and Mason let himself in, shutting the door on the miserable weather. He didn't want to take another step, worried he'd drench her hallway rug, so he stopped her there.

"I'm sorry, Joanna." It was all he could find to say.

Joanna glared at him with cold eyes. It wasn't long before her lip quivered and she fell to her knees, exhausted of all hope.

Mason had never been good at this kind of thing.

Regardless, he stepped forward and knelt by her side. "I am really sorry. I did everything I could."

"No..." Joanna sobbed. "You did not. If you'd tried —*really* tried—you'd have returned my baby girl." Her words became sniveling noises as she buried her face in her hands.

"The police will be here shortly to give you the official statement. Would you like me to wait with you until then?" On some level, he was hoping she would say no. He had his own problems to deal with.

"Get him."

"Excuse me?"

Joanna lifted her face, mascara streaming down her cheeks. "Whoever took my little girl. I want you to get him, then kill him."

Mason had dealt with reactions like this before, though it never got any easier. "I can't do that. The police have far more power. I suspect they're doing everything they—"

"Then go!" she screamed. "Go, if that's all you're good for. Just take your ass outta here!"

Standing to leave, he placed a hand on her shoulder. She shrugged it off with another sob. Mason took the hint and went for the door.

"You didn't even try," Joanna whimpered just before the door swung closed.

Stepping out into the rain, Mason trudged back to his car, not caring whether he got even more drenched. *You don't know the half of it*, he thought.

CHAPTER SIX

Mason pulled up outside his sister's apartment and shut off the engine.

"Why don't you team up with the police on this one?" Evie asked.

"The case is done. I told you, I failed."

"You know this wasn't your fault, right? What that guy did—"

"I know." Mason cut her off. He hated to think she was giving him sympathetic attention. "It's just that I'm having problems with Sandra. She kicked me out earlier."

Evie sat forward and turned to him. "Oh. I'm... Do you need somewhere to stay?"

"No. No." Mason waved his hand. "I'll head someplace else."

"You sound unsure."

Mason stared out the window at the rain. San Francisco had never looked as gloomy as it did right now. Gray clouds lurked above as the invisible sun was set of the bay. A constant drizzle patted the puddles, and the swishing of the windshield wipers was hypnotic.

"I really think you should consider it." Evie sat back, determined not to leave.

"Consider what?"

"Joining the SFPD. It's better pay, right? Some structure to help you through this difficult time? Plus, there are resources. I mean, if you're working the case anyway..."

"I'm not working the case. I told you that." Mason was riled up now. He hated being badgered into doing something he didn't want to do. At any other time in his life he may have considered going after the killer. But as long as Sandra was causing him grief, he knew he couldn't give the case his fullest attention.

"But you *should*."

Mason climbed out of the car, then walked around and opened the passenger-side door. "Good night, Evie," he said in his firmest voice, soaking in the downpour.

Evie stared at him, disbelieving, then got out and leaned in close. "Keep me in the loop," she whispered in his ear on her tiptoes, and then she was gone, leaving Mason to regret his overreaction.

With the weight of the world on his shoulders, he drove back to the office he barely used these days—the study at home made just as good an office. Inside it was cold and musty, and dust motes swirled around beneath the single dim bulb.

"What a dump," he said to himself, looking around the room. It felt like it belonged to a different man now.

He approached his liquor cabinet, took the bottle of Jack Daniels, and slumped into the clients' armchair.

Six glasses and two hours later, Mason drifted into an uncomfortable sleep, in which he saw nothing but the tears of Missy Daniels's mother and the message made from the arrangement of rocks.

None for the dame.

CHAPTER SEVEN

Mason woke up in the afternoon to a severe case of cottonmouth and a series of missed calls from Bill. *I know exactly what he's after.*

Noting the time, he sprang up and washed in the bathroom sink, then headed out of the office. For a minute he'd considered taking his car, but despite the heavy rain, he knew it was a bad idea. The alcohol was still rattling his brain.

When he arrived at the school, he waited by the buses. He probably looked suspicious, but he really didn't care. There was one thing Mason wanted, and he was going to get it.

"Dad?" Amy stepped away from the bus line, her eyes widening. She was a beautiful girl, blonde-haired and blue-eyed. Short and thin—especially for a thirteen-year-old—but not worryingly. She'd inherited none of her father's rugged features—luckily, Mason knew—nor her mom's dark-haired Mediterranean complexion.

"Hey, honey. I thought I'd walk you home. Maybe get some pizza?" He took her in his arms and waved to his daughter's friends, who'd been around for sleepovers many times in the past few years.

"Sure, Dad. Here." She popped open an umbrella and handed it to Mason, who held her close and sheltered them both as best he could.

At the pizza parlor they took a seat by the window and watched the rain hammering down. It was one of his favorite things to do.

"It's beautiful, isn't it?" Amy asked with the same enthusiasm she'd always had. She was growing up to be so bright, and Mason couldn't be more thankful she hadn't turned out like most teenagers. Not yet, at least.

"It is."

"So... pizza?" Amy asked, gesturing at the menu. "Though that's not really why you're here. Are you coming home today?"

Mason didn't know how to respond. The truth was brutal. "I should. It is my house, after all. Don't you think?"

Amy nodded, watching him, as if expecting something more.

Mason studied her expression. "You know something."

"No more than you," Amy replied. "I was on the stairs last night. I heard every word you both said. You know, it's okay to tell Mom to take a chill pill. I'll love you no matter what, Dad."

One of the things Mason loved most about his

daughter was that she always saw the more simple side of things, the type of person to look past the metaphor and cut straight to the point. "Thanks. So, has she mentioned me?"

"Who?"

"Your mom."

"Oh, no. Well..."

Mason's ears pricked up. "What?"

Amy held her temples with stiffened fingers. "She wanted to tell you in her own time."

"*What?*"

"Joshua is moving in already. That's why I want you there." She stared down at her lap. "I don't like that she's replacing you already, Dad. I don't want this."

"Wait, slow down... *Joshua* is moving in?"

"Yeah, but—"

"The fucking Pilates instructor?"

"Language, Dad." Amy had been trying to wean him out of his bad language habit lately, but it was hard to keep a lid on it right now.

"Sorry." The last thing he'd expected from today was to find out his wife had been having an affair. For now, he could try to stifle his anger, in spite of everything in his body urging him to throw a fit.

CHAPTER EIGHT

Ignoring the rain, Sandra strode down the driveway with the phone to her ear. "She's just returned. Thanks for your time." As soon as she hung up, she checked Amy was okay and sent her inside the house.

"She was with me," Mason said.

"What the *hell* do you think you're doing?"

"What am *I* doing?" he yelled. "What are *you* doing, moving a new goddamn boyfriend in already? It hasn't even been twenty-four hours!"

Sandra went red in the face as the rain matted her hair to her forehead. Her voice lowered. "I've been wanting to end this for a while."

Mason pushed past her and headed up the drive, overtaking Amy. "Is he here now?"

"Mason. No, Mason," Sandra pleaded, but with no effect.

Determined to find the guy and do him some real

damage, Mason stormed inside the house and searched from room to room while Sandra screamed at him.

"Get out or I'll call the police!"

"Sure," Mason said. "Call my ex-colleagues and tell them I've stepped foot inside my own house. Good move."

He continued scanning the rooms, but deep inside he didn't really want to find Joshua, as finding him would confirm his wife's infidelity. On the other hand, seeing him would remove all doubt, and he could no longer be played for a fool.

"He isn't here, Mason. For God's sake!" Sandra yelled at him and edged him out of the house as much as she could manage.

"Whatever." Mason was just beginning to believe her when he heard the grumble of a car's engine. A quick peek through the window revealed it to be Joshua's car. He stormed outside and marched toward it, his fists clenched into tight balls.

"Joshua!" Sandra called—a warning call that did nothing.

From the corner of his eye, Mason saw another car pull up, but he only had eyes for Joshua. Before the new boyfriend knew what was happening Mason opened the door and dragged him out. He pinned him against the side of the car and planted a fist into the guy's stomach.

Joshua let out a little *oof*.

"Stop it!" Amy yelled from somewhere behind him, but it wasn't enough.

Mason mashed the guy in the face once, twice. Each

delicious punch painted his knuckles red with nasal blood, and he felt the rage consuming him. After the fifth punch landed, he felt a strong grip around his arms as somebody pulled him back.

"Calm down, buddy. Cool it."

Joshua slumped to the floor, cowering down and holding his bloodied face.

Mason wrangled out of the grip and spun around to see Bill, realizing it must have been his car he saw pull up. "Get off me!"

"Mason. *Mason!* Calm down. Look at the girl."

Mason glanced at Amy and felt a wave of shame. Tears welled in her eyes, and she was shaking, drenched in the rain and embarrassed at the spectacle she'd just witnessed. He'd always tried to remain the more stable parent and couldn't imagine how helpless she must have felt right then.

"Come on. Let's get you out of here." Bill showed him to the car.

As they moved, Mason turned and got one last look at Sandra. She hadn't run to Mason, nor to their daughter, but to the bleeding coward on the ground who had broken up a family.

CHAPTER NINE

It was a bad time for the car to break down.

Although the rain had stopped for the first time in days, Susan Chance could see another thick cloud scudding their way. Desperately seeking help, she stepped out of the vehicle and tried to hail down one of the only cars she'd seen in the past hour.

"Please stop," she whispered to herself, thrusting her thumb out as the car sped past and splashed a puddle up at her. "Damn!"

"Mommy, I'm hungry." Tommy, her six-year-old, had cracked the window to lodge his complaint. It was as if it were the first time he'd announced it, although he'd been whining since they'd hit the road.

"I'm working on it, Tommy. Roll the window up, and wait for Mommy."

In the distance Susan spotted an RV heading their way. *Please be kind.* She waved frantically, and thanked God when the driver slowed to a stop. The rainwater on the windshield obscured her view of the driver, but she was so grateful for the help and ran to the side as the window slid down.

"Thanks so much for stopping," she said, flashing her best smile.

"No problem. You heading into the city?" The man was strange-looking, with bad teeth and thin, greasy strands of hair falling over his eyes. It wasn't an especially trustworthy face, but it was the only one around for miles.

"Yes. And... I have a young boy. I hope that's okay?"

The man stuck his head out of the window and looked over at the car.

Something didn't seem right. He looked lost in the moment, his eyes glazing over, but just as suddenly he snapped out of it. "Of course," he said. "Climb in."

Susan grabbed Tommy and left the car with the hazard lights on, hoping she could return to it soon. Thunder cracked above them as they ran back to the RV and climbed in—Tommy in the middle, as he had a totally irrational fear of sitting next to the door.

"That's it. I'll get you there safely," the man said as they drove farther down the empty road toward San Francisco.

"Thank you so much for the ride," Susan said, looking around the cab of the RV. Clipped to the rearview mirror was a photo of a young black girl. "Is she your daughter?"

The driver looked at it. "Oh. Yeah. She got her looks

from her mother. Skin color, too." He laughed. "She was black as well."

"*Was?*" Susan asked and could have slapped herself for doing so. She'd always had better manners than that. The desperation to avoid uneasy silences had taken over at that point. "I'm so sorry, I didn't mean to pry."

The man smiled that black-and-yellow grin. "It's all right. My wife died a few years back. She got the cancer, you see. It happens." His voice lacked emotion, and he wore the same offbeat expression he'd had back when he'd glanced at her car.

"Sorry to hear that," Susan said, and she could feel Tommy edging slightly over to her side. Something was wrong, but she couldn't tell what. "Would you be so kind as to drop us off at the nearest gas station?"

"Sure," the man said. "Sure. So who's this little fella?"

Lightning cracked and thunder rolled across the sky; then the rain started up again in a heavy shower. It would have been cozy if they'd been at home rather than in a stranger's RV. "This is Tommy. Say hi, Tommy."

But Tommy was too shy—or too scared—to answer, and it was hard to tell which. He only buried his face into his mother's sweater.

"Well, don't be shy, boy," the driver told him. "I ain't gonna bite ya."

"Hello." Tommy croaked it rather than said it, but it was better than no attempt at all.

"You like the rain, boy?"

"Not really." Tommy giggled awkwardly.

"Me neither. Makes everything squidgy." The driver fell silent then, like he was focusing on the road.

Trying to figure out how far along the route they were, Susan peered through the glass to catch a look at the signs, but it was impossible with the storm blurring the scenery.

"What's this?" Tommy picked up a small jade hairclip from between the seats.

"That?" The driver snatched it from him and threw it onto the dashboard. "That's nothing. My damn wife keeps leaving things lying around."

Susan's eyes widened with alarm. "You said your wife had passed."

"Hmm? Oh, she did. I meant she *kept* leaving things lying around. I don't have too many people ride up front with me, so nobody tends to tell me about the mess."

Susan could hear the engine revving up and the needle on the speedometer flicking over. "Could you slow down, please? I think there's a gas station if you turn right here."

"Sure," the driver said, but he didn't slow down at all.

Susan watched as he sped toward the crossroad, which led down into the city to the right. The left fork, however, led up into the woods.

Ignoring her directions, the driver turned left.

CHAPTER TEN

"Sir, I think we're going the wrong way."

The driver said nothing but kept on driving toward the forest, where a number of horror stories had supplied the citizens of San Francisco with endless rumors and campfire stories.

"Sir, I—"

"Just shut your damn hole, will ya?" the man snapped, and he pulled out a pistol.

Susan recoiled, and Tommy leaned into her. It wasn't the first time she'd seen a gun, but it was certainly the first time one had been pointed at her. "Please, don't hurt us. We just want our car working again. If you let us out now, we won't tell anyone. I promise."

"Stop your moaning, woman. Have some backbone."

"But—"

"Another word and I'll shoot you dead, you hear?"

He drove them farther into the hills, where he eventually stopped on a dark stretch of road that split the forest. There was an undeniable feeling of loneliness and seclusion up here. And rightfully so; they were completely alone.

"Please..."

The driver shut off the engine and aimed the gun at Susan's face. "Get out."

She hesitated. "W-What?"

"You heard me."

Susan fumbled for the door handle and almost fell out as she opened it. The rain hit her hard and fast, instantly soaking her through. Trembling, she held her hands out toward her son, helping him out of the RV.

"No." The driver pulled back on the hammer of the gun. "Leave the boy."

Susan couldn't help crying. She'd always dreaded the thought of somebody taking her boy away, and she wouldn't let him go. "Please, I need my son."

"I need him more, bitch. Now close the door, or I'll shoot the pair of you."

Susan shook her head slowly, looking at Tommy's terrified expression. "Please."

"Last chance," the driver said, clutching Tommy's raincoat.

"Mommy," Tommy whined.

"I'm sorry, baby," Susan said, and she closed the door.

The RV's wheels spun and flicked up dirt and gravel as they pulled away, leaving Susan Chance alone in the darkness while her son was taken away by the stranger.

If Robert were around, she thought, *this never would have happened.*

Susan despised herself, crying and shaking in the rain.

Alone.

CHAPTER ELEVEN

Mason had accepted their meal with grace, but it still felt like a bribe. Bill's wife, Christine, had been kind enough to cook dinner, while Bill made small talk until they were done.

"I'll just clear these up." Christine collected the empty plates and headed for the kitchen.

"Allow me," Mason said, but Bill demanded that he sit.

When they were alone, Bill leaned back in his chair and retrieved a key from a nearby drawer. He threw it to Mason, who caught it with one deft flick of the hand. "That's yours."

"For what?"

"You're staying with us," Bill said, as if it weren't a choice. "And you'll be working the case whether you like it or not."

"Bill, I—"

"The Lullaby Killer is back, Mason. There's no

running from it anymore. Now, you can sit around all day and mope about losing your wife to that asshole Joshua, or you can get to work. You're more familiar with this guy than anyone at the station."

"So? Read the file and you'll know everything I know." Mason felt like an ungrateful son of a bitch, and it wasn't how he'd intended to sound. Regardless, he wouldn't be pushed into a corner.

"You owe us, Mason. You owe me."

"I don't owe you a damn thing."

Bill shoved back his chair and stormed into another room. Moments later he returned with a photo frame, dumping it into Mason's lap. "Look at it."

Mason knew exactly what it was, and he knew it would win him over. Still, he couldn't help but look. In his lap was the photograph of Michael—Bill and Christine's son. He was sitting on Bill's shoulders with a big, cheesy grin on his face.

"It's two years since that psychopath took our son, but we still feel it every day. I suppose I don't need to remind you who was working the case."

Mason lowered the photo, then looked up at Bill.

"My son—your godson—died because of him. So what if he's been quiet ever since? What difference does time make? The fact is he's still out there, and you're sitting here whining about how *your* family is falling apart. Now, I can put you up here, Mason. You're welcome to stay as long as you like. That one comes for free, whatever you do. But you and I both know you need to take this case."

The room fell silent, the only sound the rhythmic tick-tock of a clock adding to the tension. Christine could no longer be heard clattering dishes in the kitchen: it was obvious she'd been listening to all the yelling.

"Please, Mason."

Mason took a deep breath. He thought of Amy. There were other kids out there, he knew, who were just like her. And for as long as this killer was on the streets, those kids would be in danger.

"Let me sleep on it."

CHAPTER TWELVE

It was barely sunrise, and Bill had practically dragged Mason to the police station on the basis that it was "an emergency." Mason soon believed it, especially when he was shown into the viewers' booth behind the interview room.

Susan Chance sat at the table, a perfectly average woman in most ways aside from being drenched and caked in mud and with nothing but a towel over her shoulders. Her makeup had run down her pale cheeks, and she looked a mess. Mason didn't need a PhD in psychology to know the woman had been through hell and back.

"Can you tell us more about the photograph?" Bill asked her.

Mason studied her reaction through the glass: nothing short of horror.

"It was a black girl." Susan sniffed. "Ten, maybe younger."

"Can you please take a look at this picture?" Bill slid a photograph across the table.

Susan wiped her nose with a bare arm and took the photo.

"Is this the photograph that was clipped to his mirror?"

"Yes." Susan's eyes lit up in horror. "I mean no. It's the same girl but a different photo. Who is she?"

"That's Missy Daniels," Bill told her in a soft voice, putting the photo aside. Mason knew exactly why he didn't add, "and she was murdered two days ago."

"What about the man?" Bill went on. He'd always been a very competent detective, his efforts only overshadowed by Mason's accomplishments. And although Mason didn't revel in the glory, neither did Bill Harvey hold it against him. In fact, he'd actually claimed to admire him.

"Only what I already told you. But..."

"Yes?"

"His hands..." Susan burst into floods of tears, unable to speak, and Mason could feel his heart breaking along with hers. With a daughter of his own, he could only imagine how utterly distraught she was.

"Please stay with me, Mrs. Chance. What about his hands?"

"Gloves," she finally said, demonstrating with spread fingers. "He was wearing leather gloves."

This seemed perfectly natural to Mason, even considering the time of year. If *he* were to kidnap somebody's boy, he would probably wear gloves, too. In fact, he'd have taken every precaution possible to not get caught.

After the interview, Bill met Mason in the corridor. "What do you make of that?"

"It doesn't sound like him," Mason said. "He wouldn't show his face like that."

"Can you be sure?"

"Not really. But if it *is* him, the kid will show up in a couple of days."

"That'll be too late," Bill said.

"No kidding."

They moved to one side to allow other officers to hustle past them. "So, what do you think? Can you help us?"

Mason sighed. "I have conditions."

"Shoot."

"I want all the info as it comes in. *As it comes in*, and not a second later. I want immediate access to every crime scene, no evidence withheld. No exceptions."

"All right. Is that it?" Bill sighed, satisfied.

"No. I want the police to stay out of my way. I'm working independently on this one."

Bill paused and swallowed, then answered. "You got it. Thanks, Mason."

Before they got the chance to shake on it, Captain Leanne Cox passed them, surrounded by a small team. She gave an approving nod. "Mr. Black," she said. "Welcome back to the team."

As Mason opened his mouth to stress he was working as an external party, she was already headed out the door.

Bill stood smiling at him. "Come on."

CHAPTER THIRTEEN

The first thing Mason did was take a cab back to his office. If he was going to work the case, he would need a few things to get ahead.

He started with a clean suit and his PI badge. Next he opened the drawer to grab his gun but thought better of it. In the past, that thing had caused more trouble than it had solved, and he was in no state to be taking shots at people.

Just as he was grabbing his jacket to leave, Evie let herself into the building, walked over, and wrapped her arms around his hulking frame. "I heard about the fight. I'm so sorry."

Mason stood without moving his arms. That had always been his way.

"Are you okay? Have you found someplace to stay?" she asked with the all-too-familiar tone of their mother.

"I'm fine. Bill's putting me up for a while."

"Great. That's great. And the case?"

Mason stepped back and looked at her. "What exactly are you after?"

"What? I'm just asking if you're working again. Cut me some slack."

Mason sighed and shoved his arms into the jacket sleeves. "Yes, I'm working the case."

"Fantastic! Let me help."

"No, Evie. This is exactly what I was worried about." Mason's pulse quickened. "I know you hate it when I call you *the press*, but that's what you are. That's at least one of your interests in this, if not the biggest."

Evie looked around and let out a breath. "I guess you're right. But maybe we could help each other out."

Mason snatched up the keys to his Mustang and switched off the office lights with a grunt. "How could you possibly help?"

"Think about it. I could help you by running whatever errands you need, and you can reward me with information. And I'll only print what you give me permission to print."

"It's no good, Evie. I can't allow that." Mason opened the door and ushered her out.

"Well, what's your plan, then?" Evie asked, talking fast as she usually did when desperate.

"Excuse me?"

"What's your first step?"

Mason was speechless. He hadn't actually formulated a plan, other than to go over the files one more time until something popped out.

"That's what I thought," Evie said, grinning. "But I

just happen to know that Missy Daniels went to school with Tommy Chance."

"The missing kid?"

Evie nodded, her expression smug.

"How'd you know about that?" This was exactly what pissed him off. He'd only known about the abduction for a couple of hours, and it'd been leaked to her already. If he was lucky, it wouldn't be on her website yet.

"I have my ways. So, maybe we could check out the school together. What do you say?"

Mason held the door. *I suppose a partner could be useful*, he thought. *As long as she doesn't get herself hurt.* "Fine. But you print *nothing* until I give you clearance. If I say jump, you ask how high. Got it?"

"Got it." She hadn't smiled this much in a long time.

Mason hated it. "Get in the car."

CHAPTER FOURTEEN

The killer knew from experience that the longer he kept these kids, the more risk there was of being caught. That was why he'd planned his trip to the Muir Woods National Park beforehand. He had all the tools in his RV.

He followed the trail halfway up, with little Tommy Chance walking by his side, minus a finger. Cruel or not—he knew very well it was—there was something satisfying about snipping off the pinkie.

"Where are we going?" Tommy asked in a whimper.

"What'd I tell ya, boy? Shut up, or I'll make it hurt."

The heavy bag on his back was already giving him enough trouble. He had a large range of tools inside: hammer, chisel, pliers, and a whole bunch of other useful things.

When they reached a split in the path, the killer went straight on and through the trees, dragging the boy behind him. The torrential rain had created a treacherous trail, but there was enough decaying tree mulch to grip to.

After a steep ten-minute hike, they stopped.

"Right here."

The boy was trembling as the Lullaby Killer dropped the bag, opened it up, removed a rope, and tossed it over. "Put your head through the loop."

The boy hesitated, sobbing and pleading with his eyes.

"I won't ask again."

Tommy slipped the rope around his neck and gawped anxiously at the snaking end as the killer took it and tied it securely around a huge rock.

"I think that should do it, don't you?" He loved every moment of this—everything from the clean slice of the finger to the terrified look in the boy's eyes. Trembling with anticipation, he knelt and removed the hammer and chisel.

"Excuse me."

The voice startled him, a wave of heat surging down his neck. He spun around and saw a young man with long, wavy hair, one of the surfer types you saw in the movies. His eyes were accusing, looking from the killer to little Tommy and back again.

"Hey, what the hell's going on here?" the man asked, stepping forward.

The Lullaby Killer smiled. "We're just playing a game. Ain't that right, boy?"

Tommy nodded, still crying. Even *he* was bright enough not to scream for help.

"It doesn't look like a game to me. Sir, step away." The man took a cell phone from his pocket and began to dial—probably for the police.

Acting on instinct, the killer tightened his grip on the hammer's hilt and smashed it across the man's temple. It made an exhilarating *thump*, and the man hit the leaves a second later. *You can't be sure about these things*, he thought, and the killer crouched and delivered two more bone-crushing blows to the man's face until it was nothing more than tenderizing a juicy steak.

Shaking with adrenaline, the killer stood, wiping traces of spattered blood from his face with his sleeve as he turned to the boy. It didn't look like he was strong enough to move the rock, and his hands were bound, so he wouldn't be undoing the knots anytime soon. With that in mind, the killer dragged the man away by his feet, scooped up his cell phone, then covered him in a mass of wet leaves and dirt sods.

Checking the phone, the killer's heart began pounding like crazy as he saw pictures of him leaving his RV.

He knew he had to destroy the evidence, and he thought of his sweet spot underneath the RV's tire. All he had to do first was finish his work with the kid, then carve a message into a nearby tree.

And move on to find his next victim.

CHAPTER FIFTEEN

The school's principal was a petite, polite lady with kind features. She seemed busy, but not so much that she couldn't take time out of her day for a good cause.

"Thanks for seeing us," Mason said, leading the charge as they were shown into the office. Everything inside was made of oak, and the greenery added a touch of hominess to the space.

"Absolutely." She gestured to a seat. "What can I do for you?"

"We're to understand that Missy Daniels was a student here?" Mason laced his fingers. He'd never had any need for a notepad; the map in his head served as a better guide.

"Oh, yes. Such a shame what happened to her. We'll be mourning her for a long, long time." She lowered her head in theatrical sadness.

Mason tried to disguise his amusement at her effort.

Evie took the reins. "And Thomas Chance?"

"Thomas Chance... Thomas Ch—Ah, yes! He is absent today, if I recall."

Evie looked to Mason, who took a breath. "Thomas was abducted yesterday. We're here to see if you know any reason why this school may be targeted. Have you seen anyone suspicious, or have the children been spreading any rumors?"

"Rumors?" The principal shook her head, her mouth open and her gaze wandering. "Not that I'm aware of. Is this a police investigation?"

"We're private investigators working closely with the SFPD, ma'am, and we do appreciate your cooperation in the matter." This was often the part where he'd be told to go fuck himself. Thankfully, this woman seemed eager to be of use.

"Well, there's a substitute teacher who a few of us are suspicious of. Charlie Richards, his name is. He hasn't necessarily done anything wrong, but he has, well... there's a certain coldness about him, you see."

Evie remained silent, while Mason wondered how far a simple judgment could take them.

"The reason I bring it up," she went on, "is because he was supposed to be here yesterday, but called in sick. Said he had some sort of flu, but it sounded exaggerated."

Mason felt that old excitement swelling inside him again—the stuff that had made him enjoy his work back when he was a detective. "Could you please supply his address?"

"I'm afraid I'm not at liberty to disclose that information." The principal stood, her frail frame edging slowly away from the desk. "However, if I turn my head for a moment, you can see yourselves out?" She pushed a folder across the desk and smiled.

"Thank you for your time," Evie said, grinning.

As soon as the door clicked shut, Evie was on her feet and flicking through the pages to find Charlie Richards. "Got it," she said, her eyes lighting up.

But Mason's attention had turned to his phone, reading a new message carefully.

"What is it?"

"There's been another murder," he said, his voice flat and miserable.

"Is it Tommy Chance?"

"I don't know. Apparently he's left a message, so it could be."

Evie sighed. "All right. You head to the scene, and I'll check out this Charlie guy."

"No!" Mason could not have been firmer. "I'll have you at my side, but you can't go running off to interview a suspect. It might not be safe."

Evie lifted the leg of her pants to reveal a pocketknife in a shin strap. Mason had bought it for her the previous Christmas and had it engraved. He'd not seen it since then but was amazed to see she was putting it to use, even if as a precautionary measure.

"You suspect *anything*, you let me know," Mason demanded.

"I can take care of myself." Evie led them out of the room.

Mason had seen that kind of overconfidence before, and it had gotten them in trouble on more than one occasion—both of them.

Somehow, he got the feeling this would be one of those times.

CHAPTER SIXTEEN

Mason stopped in the parking lot and slogged his way up the hill beneath a relentless rain. A sickness started roiling in his stomach as he braced himself for what he was about to see.

"That was fast," Bill said, meeting him at the top of the slope.

Mason caught up to him, panting. He was in good shape—*great* shape, actually—but it was still an exhausting climb. "What do you have for me?"

Bill led him over to the body, a pale-faced young boy hanging from a tree. Blood streamed from the sockets of his crow-pecked eyes, making the face difficult to identify. Mason pictured Susan, the boy's mother, and how she'd cried before. He didn't want to imagine how much this would hurt her, and prayed this wasn't her son.

"Christ," he said.

"Exactly."

"You said there's a message?"

Bill led him to a nearby tree, where the words had been carved into the bark: *CRADLE AND ALL*. It was sloppy work. The killer had been in a rush.

"Sorry to keep asking, but you think it's a clue?"

"Sorry to keep telling you, but it's nothing more than a brag-tag. These sickos can't help themselves. Sometimes they just need the approval. Like when you do something good for someone else and it's really for yourself, but you still want a pat on the back."

"Excuse me, Detective Harvey?" A uniformed young officer appeared at Bill's side and removed his cap. "There's been an ID on the body. It's Thomas Chance, sir."

"The prints match?" Bill asked.

Mason didn't want to hear this conversation. Instead, he followed the breadcrumbs in his head. If the killer had been in a hurry, as the scruffy chiseling suggested, then he must have made a slipup somewhere.

Staying focused, Mason walked the perimeter of the scene in search of additional clues. Everything was so wet and covered in filth it was hard to make out much of anything. But one thing did catch his eye, and he couldn't have ignored it even if he'd wanted to.

"Mason?" Bill called from somewhere behind him.

But Mason was in his zone, following what looked like a drag path. Deep grooves had been scraped into the mud, and he followed the trail into the trees until they stopped.

"What is it?" Bill asked, following him.

Something wasn't right here, there was no doubt

about it. Mason dropped to his knees and swiped away the clot of wet leaves, ignoring the dirt that was accumulating on his pant legs. As he made his fourth swipe, he felt something hard and knew what it was.

The face was barely uncovered before it emitted a sickening smell. Mason wiped off the last of the leaves to reveal a bloody, horrific mess. Flies buzzed in a swarm around him, lured in by the foul odor.

Mason dug his mouth into his sleeve and tried not to gag.

"Forensics!" Bill yelled, holding back his own bile. "We need forensics!"

CHAPTER SEVENTEEN

"What about the man?" Mason asked as he rapped on Susan Chance's front door. He dreaded having to tell her the devastating news, but at least his friend was at his side. "Who was he?"

"He's still being identified," Bill said. "You'll know when I do."

The door sprang open and Susan glanced at them both before waving them in. She was about to sit down but seemed to think better of it when Mason and Bill entered the room and offered a look of remorse.

"What's... Is something wrong?" she asked.

"I'm so sorry," Bill said.

Mason hadn't heard him this upset since his own son had been taken.

"No." Susan shook her head. She looked exactly as she had when Mason had last seen her, only her eyes had become red and sore, as if she'd been rubbing them. "No.

You were supposed to help. You were supposed to save my little boy!"

No matter what we do, Mason thought, *no matter how much we sacrifice to get the job done, we're always the ones to blame.*

Susan stepped forward and pushed Bill with surprising strength. Mason couldn't help but wonder where that strength was when the man had pulled a gun on her and her son. He stepped forward and took her arms, guiding her into a nearby chair.

Bill retreated to the corner of the room, where he stood looking distraught.

"I'm so... We are so sorry, Mrs. Chance." Mason had difficulty finding his words. "We did everything we could, but there... there just wasn't enough time."

"You failed," she spat, staring at Bill. "I trusted you to help him, but you failed."

"Now, that's not fair. We've not even known about him for a whole day yet, and—"

Susan stood and shoved past Mason. She wasn't quite strong enough to move him, but he stepped aside in time to allow her room. She went to the desk and opened a drawer, and for a moment Mason thought she was going to show them a picture of the boy, use it as emotional blackmail to try to undo the damage.

But when she turned with the revolver in her hand, everything changed.

Bill drew his own sidearm with lightning speed, aiming directly at her. "Drop it."

Mason suddenly regretted having left his gun at

home. He also had a spare pistol in the glove compartment, but he hadn't thought he'd need it. It was strictly for emergencies. "Calm down, Mrs. Chance. That won't help."

Susan turned the gun from Mason to Bill. She was grinding her teeth, overwrought with rage and heartache. Mason understood her; she wanted someone to blame. She only wanted a reason why this happened.

"You..." She shifted it back to Mason, her cheeks reddening and tears filling her eyes.

"Drop the weapon now!" Bill yelled, ruining Mason's attempt to calm her down. "I don't want to shoot you, Mrs. Chance, but I'll have no choice unless you drop the gun."

There was a whirlwind in Susan's eyes as she paused to consider her options. And then there was recognition, as she seemed to understand the only true way of ending her pain.

In the blink of an eye, she put the barrel of the gun in her mouth.

"Don't—" Mason screamed, but his words were interrupted by the blast of the revolver and the spray of scarlet on the wall behind Susan Chance.

CHAPTER EIGHTEEN

Evie climbed out of the cab and asked the driver to wait. She was looking at a rundown cesspool of a house, clearly suffering from a lack of attention. The windows were boarded, and the paint was flaking off. The smell also didn't go unnoticed—something stale.

Trying not to breathe in too much of the stench, she approached the door and gave it a knock. She peered through the glass, but it appeared empty inside. No movement, no light; everything to suggest she should exercise caution.

"Can I help you?" a man said in a strong British accent from behind. It wasn't the posh, stereotypical accent normally associated with England—more like a rough cockney.

Evie turned to look at the man, a lean guy with a shaved head and glasses. His mouth hung open with distaste, and his dentistry met the perceived cliché. "Hi. My name's Evie Black. I'm looking for Charlie Richards."

The man studied her for a moment. "What's this about?"

"I want to talk to you about the disappearance of a young boy. Thomas Chance. He was one of your students?"

"Oh, 'ere we bloody go. Every time anything goes wrong in this bloody country, everyone looks to the immigrant. I swear to God, I'm gonna complain to the EFT about this." The man moved quickly to the front door and fumbled his keys into the lock.

"Sir, can I just have a moment?" Evie asked in desperation.

"No."

"Fine, then I'll print some nasty stuff about you anyway."

Charlie stopped then, a contemplative look on his face as he turned. "Journalist?"

"Of sorts." Evie shrugged. "Look, Thomas Chance was abducted yesterday afternoon. We spoke to your employer, who said you'd phoned in sick. Where were you?"

A resigned sigh escaped his lips, and he stepped back onto the porch, looking nervously up and down the street. "I'll tell you what I was doing, but I want your word that you won't let any of this get out. If it does, I'll lose my job."

Evie had that feeling you sometimes get when you're hungry and you catch a tantalizing whiff of hot food. It was a tedious longing. "I swear, it's between you and me."

"All right." Charlie looked down at his feet. "I was with a woman."

"I don't understand. Why would that cost you your job?"

"She was... you know..."

Evie's mouth hung open, and she shook her head. *Why so evasive?*

"She was... a hooker."

"Oh."

"But you promised. You swore you wouldn't repeat this."

"And I won't. But how can I credit this? Do you have any proof?"

"I'm his proof, darling." A new voice from somewhere behind them.

Evie turned to the source of the voice and saw a slender Asian woman approaching the house, looking down her nose at Evie and heading inside. She wore denim shorts and a low-cut top under an open jacket that let almost everything hang out. Whatever this woman was paid to perform, it wasn't discretion.

"Miss Black, I don't want you coming 'raand here again. You got it?" Charlie let the hooker inside and didn't wait for an answer before slamming the door in Evie's face.

With nobody to speak to and no more leads to follow, Evie headed back down the path toward the cab, mumbling "Goddamnit" under her breath.

CHAPTER NINETEEN

It was late afternoon, and school was finishing up. A perfect time to hunt.

The Lullaby Killer had considered waiting it out, giving it a few days before he struck again, but the thirst was more powerful than ever. Although debating it in his head, he'd managed to convince himself that it wouldn't hurt to window-shop.

He took the RV down Waylard Road, watching all the kids returning from school. Before long, they would drop off their bags at home and announce they were heading over to their friends' houses. It would then be normal not to hear from them for hours. That was when the killer would take what he needed and get out of there.

No, don't. Be on your best behavior. Just for a little while.

Why though? The police are clueless.

But Mr. Black isn't, he reminded himself.

That was the difference with the detective; he was the one sheep in the herd that refused to follow. This Mason Black person was far too involved for the killer's liking, but what could he do? He'd almost caught him before, until he'd simply quit his job.

That's dedication, huh?

The killer drove down the street, the rain stopping just long enough for a gust of wind to lift the matted leaves off the ground. They swirled through the air and came at the windshield of his RV in a flurry, distracting him.

Maybe the school is your best bet, the tormenting voice in his head teased.

No, you shouldn't.

But please do.

The withdrawal was aching. It'd been less than a couple hours, and he already wanted to hear the desperate cries of some small child, some privileged little bastard who thought the world of himself while all the parents and teachers kissed his ass. It was a load of bullshit, of course—he would grow up and follow the system, settling for a crappy job in a bank or at a law firm, paying taxes and getting married like every other sheep in America.

This country is bullshit. These people are bullshit.

On the other hand, he could take a girl. Some pretty little thing who would only grow up to upset her father and break some poor guy's heart. He knew they could be real sluts, those women. Never for him—they were too picky—but they were sluts to other men, and nothing made him angrier.

The killer drove on, still fighting his urges.

Do it.

Don't.

Do it.

CHAPTER TWENTY

Mason was discharged after leaving his statement and headed straight to Downadays Bar to meet Evie. It had been their favorite place to drink for years now, a quiet little spot in an even quieter location. The music was mediocre and the food ordinary, but the service was good and the drinks were cheap. What else mattered?

Evie was waiting for him when he pulled up. Her hair was down, and her eyes had dark bags beneath them. She definitely needed sleep.

"Took your time," she said.

"I had some things to do," Mason retorted, stalking across the lot.

"Some things?"

"Yeah, some things."

The moment he opened the door, they were assaulted by blaring youthful music. It was awful—some high-pitched guy singing about how a woman had let him down—but at least it had an upbeat rhythm. They took a seat at the bar, Mason dumping a file in front of him and Evie removing her purse from her shoulder.

"So, did you talk to the teacher?" Mason asked, signaling for two beers.

"Dead end. How'd things go at the crime scene?"

"Actually, we found a body."

"Well, duh."

"No, I mean we found *another* body. A hidden one." Mason shoved the file her way.

Evie flipped it open and looked at the picture of a man. "You got an ID already?"

"Sure did. His wife is on her way back from New York right now. I'm collecting her from the airport tomorrow morning. I'll weave in my interview during the journey."

"That's how I know you're my brother," Evie said, looking up with a grin.

Two bottles of beer appeared in front of them, and Mason handed over some cash. "You're welcome to publish that. A gift, from me to you."

Evie beamed. "You're sure?"

Mason nodded.

"Mase..."

"Don't call me that. You know I hate it." He took a long slug of his beer.

"Well then, *Mason*, did you talk to Sandra yet?"

"No, and I have no intention to."

Evie closed the file and twisted in her chair to look at him. "Listen, I won't tell you what to do. But I will say that if I were you, I would make my feelings known. Nothing aggressive, just one adult to another. At least then I'd be able to see Amy."

Mason drank the rest of his beer, trying not to think about his daughter. The last thing he needed right now was to be reminded of his family—or lack thereof.

"Hey, sweetness." A man appeared to Evie's right side. He was scruffy. Stocky, but not tall. He hadn't shaved, and his hair was far too greasy to go unnoticed. "How 'bout I buy you a drink or two, and then you can come back to my place?"

Mason just stared at him.

"No, thank you," Evie said.

"Aw, come on. You don't gotta be like that," the drunk said, looking her up and down.

Evie turned in her chair. "Look, I don't mean to be rude, but I'm here to discuss work with my brother. So, if you wouldn't mind, I'd like to get back to it."

Just as she was turning back, he grabbed her wrist.

Mason shot to his feet and stepped around Evie, grabbing at the man's coat and pulling him forward. He was lighter than Mason had expected. "Keep your dirty little mitts to yourself."

The drunk gawped at him, obviously intimidated. After being silenced for a few seconds, he cleared his throat. "Whatever. Bitch probably got crabs anyway."

Mason shrugged him off and watched him leave.

"Some people, huh?" Evie laughed.

"It's not funny. People like that don't know what *no* means."

"Relax. He's not the first creep to try it on with me."

Over the next hour or so, they discussed the case and caught up on the day's events, and when done Mason tipped the bartender as they headed for the door. They were making their way to the Mustang when Mason heard footsteps behind him.

But he was a second too late.

"Yo, big guy." It was the slurring drunk, and he was swinging an iron pole.

Mason turned and raised his wrist in time to block it, but it rattled his arm and he cried out in agony. There were more of them this time. Three, it seemed, in the haze of adrenaline. One of them grabbed at Evie, and she wriggled and squirmed.

Mason's arm was on fire with pain as he saw a lazy haymaker coming his way. He ducked, dropped to a knee, and punched as hard as he could into the guy's balls. Mason knew it was a temporary stun at best, so he shot back to his feet, grabbed the man's head, and drove his knee upward into the man's nose.

The drunk was too stunned to react and fell onto his back with a crippled moan. One of the other thugs stepped forward. Mason glanced right to ensure Evie hadn't been hurt.

But she was doing better than he was.

She was holding her knife in a steady fist and even stood in the stance Mason had taught her. She and the assailant were both poised, one ready to attack, the other preparing to defend, and both were figuring out which was which.

The second guy went for Mason, landing a sucker punch on his eye. It rocked him, but not enough to bring him down. After all, Mason had more than a few inches on him. Assessing the guy's weight, Mason stomped forward and shot a left jab at the man's rib cage, then quickly lifted him by his throat with his right hand. He came off the ground with ease, and Mason brought him down even easier.

There was an audible crunch when his spine hit the ground.

Evie.

Mason turned to his sister, who was being closed in on. Unprepared to let his sister get hurt, he dashed forward and grabbed the guy, pinning him against the Mustang. He hadn't realized his friends had been taken down, because when he saw them he stopped resisting and let go of Mason's arms.

"You picked the wrong day to fuck with us," Mason hissed through gritted teeth. "You give me one goddamn reason why I shouldn't rip your head off right now."

"Mason," Evie said, lowering the knife.

"Please," the guy begged, choking.

"One fucking reason!" Mason couldn't control himself, the red mist rising.

Joshua taking his wife; the Lullaby Killer returning to wreak havoc; now these assholes trying to hurt his sister.

He was a man on the brink.

"Mason!" Evie yelled, snapping him back into the moment.

Mason swung the guy around and kicked him up the

ass to encourage a swift departure, his blood still boiling as he tried to recover his breath. "Get the hell out of here, and call an ambulance for your little buddies."

"It's all right," Evie said when they were alone. "Are you okay?"

"I'm fine," Mason said, wincing at the pain in his arm. "It's you I'm worried about. I told you there're people like this out there."

Evie put a hand on her hip. "And you just thought you'd be a hero, huh?"

There was silence before the clouds rolled into each other, making the sky grumble its own anger.

"I know what this is about," she went on.

"You do?"

"Of course. After the way mom and dad died, you feel as if you have to protect your sister. But I'm doing just fine. I really am. Look, you need to get some rest. It's a big day tomorrow, right?"

Mason was too pissed off to argue. "Right. Let's go."

They climbed into the car and drove off, leaving the thug whimpering to the 911 dispatch, standing over his friends' unconscious, battered bodies.

CHAPTER TWENTY-ONE

Mrs. Sampson was a tall woman, and much younger than expected. She walked out of the arrival gate with a suitcase in tow and a lost expression on her face. That was, until she read the card with her name on it.

"Mrs. Sampson? I'm Mason Black, your escort."

She offered a smile, no matter how forced. "The detective I spoke to on the phone?"

"Well, no," he said. "That was my contact, Bill Harvey." Mason wanted to tell her that he was only a PI; that helpful dose of honesty was always nice to get out of the way. But when it wasn't necessary, like right now, he didn't see much point. Besides, the longer she thought he was a cop, the more information she'd be willing to give. "I'm so sorry about what's happened. If there's anything I can do—"

"Just the ride home," she said. "And please, call me Mandy."

Mason showed her to his Mustang, addressing her worried look by telling her he was a slow driver. Most people reacted the same when they got into his car, climbing in with a look of curious anticipation, but leaving with a pale face and shaky legs.

"So, Mandy, I want to ask some questions about your husband, if that's okay? Anything you don't want to tell me, you're not obligated to answer. And if you'd like a break, don't be too shy to stop me."

Mandy adjusted her position as they drove away from the airport, and turned her face away, probably to hide her sadness. "Anything I can do to help. We have to pass the time somehow, right?"

Mason smiled at her charm and admired her courage. Most people would have been in pieces by now. "When did you last hear from your husband? Did you know he was going up the trail?"

"Sure I knew," she said. "He called me beforehand."

"From home?"

"From the parking lot at the base of the trail."

Mason knew the spot from when he'd parked there yesterday. *But that means...* "He called you from a cell phone?" He had difficulty focusing on the road with his heart beating so fast.

"Yeah. He said he saw somebody suspicious... a man with a crying child. He called me for advice, seeing if he had a right to intervene. I told him to stay away, but..." Mandy's voice cracked, and she wafted air at her eyes.

Mason glanced over at her, watching her dry her eyes. *Could that have been the killer?* He said nothing, letting her decide for herself whether to carry on talking. He turned back to the road.

"He followed anyway," Mandy continued.

"Mrs. Sampson, no cell phone was recovered from the crime scene."

She looked right at him, and a quick glance told him that her makeup was a runny mess. He opened the glove compartment, rifled through the paperwork and spare gun, and plucked out a pack of tissues and handed them to her.

"Thank you." She blew her nose. "But there must be some mistake. He definitely had his cell on him."

Mason thought hard. "What's the betting that if I find that phone, I'll find something on it?"

"James was a careful man. I wouldn't put it past him to have taken a photo or two. Keep it for evidence if you need it. I have no use for it."

"You're very kind, Mrs. Sampson."

"Mandy," she corrected again.

Mason drove her home and walked her to the door. The police would be around soon, but at least he'd gotten what he needed from her, and he'd gotten it quicker than they ever would have. He left his card with her, and she wished him luck in finding the killer.

Mason got back in his car and sped off to the crime scene.

Finally, he thought, *a missing detail that might lead to a clue.*

CHAPTER TWENTY-TWO

It was dusk when Mason arrived, and the parking lot was empty. It was eerie, but worth the possibility of finding something.

Using the flashlight on his phone, he stumbled back up the trail, ducking into the row of trees where the path split in two. It was odd positioning for a murder scene; just out of the way enough so not everyone would see it, but still not too hard to find.

Rummaging through the growing darkness, Mason followed the tracks back to where the man had been found. He tried hard not to look at the tree where the body of little Thomas Chance had been hanging only a day ago. The image sickened him.

How many more children have to die before I find this son of a bitch?

Mason reached the clearing, scanning the ground for the missing cell phone. It could have been anywhere around the area, if it hadn't already been stamped into the mud, then picked up by a kid who lucked into finding a lost phone. Mason only hoped that if someone had taken it, they would soon hand it in to the police.

But as past experience told him, that rarely happened.

Giving up on his search, he hustled back down the path to the parking lot. He was just about to call it a day, had even pulled the keys from his pocket, when something occurred to him. Above him, attached to a lamppost, a security camera was pointing down. The police had checked the tapes but had found nothing.

But the camera wasn't pointed at the protected parking area.

It was a small shelter, made of old, thin wood, perhaps wide enough for six or seven cars though the ground wasn't marked for them. Mason glanced around inside the dark area, looking up for a camera. Again, there was nothing.

He shone the flashlight down, and now something caught his eye. Minding his step, he approached and kneeled to find the remains of a crumpled cell phone. It looked as if it was beyond repair, but at least it hadn't suffered any water damage—the shelter had seen to that.

Mason snagged an evidence bag from his coat pocket, turned it inside out, and scooped the wrecked phone into it. If he could get this back to the tech team at SFPD, he might have a chance of recovering any data from it.

That was, *if* he got lucky.

CHAPTER TWENTY-THREE

Evie Black preferred to work from home. It was a safe haven, with no distractions.

She'd been typing up all the details, arranging them into an order that would make sense to a reader—as she'd trained for during her many journalism courses. She scanned in the pictures, attaching some with a warning that the gore might make some people uneasy. In spite of her experience with such matters, it even made *her* feel sick.

She was just finishing up when she received the email from *BRAHM82*. Her fingers finished typing the blog as if on autopilot, while her eyes fixed on that name. *Do I know this person?* She thought not, but on the suspicion that it might be fan mail caressing her ego, she couldn't wait to open it.

That was her first mistake.

Her eyes scanned over the threat as her heart lodged in her throat.

Miss Black,

You've been working too hard on this case over the years. As fascinating as it has been to read about your findings, might I dissuade you from delving any further into the matter? Think, for instance, if anything happened to Amelia...

I'll be watching.
    Brahm

P.S. If this email gets out, I'll know.

Evie's heart beat like a drum while she read and reread the email.

Who the hell is this guy? How does he know about Amelia? Amelia was her biggest secret. She'd only ever told one person about her, and that was Mason. It didn't even cross her mind that he might have something to do with this. Sure, he could be a little aggressive sometimes, but not toward her, and never without provocation.

As painful as it was, Evie decided it was better not to cause further risk, and deleted the post—her pride vanishing with it. She headed to bed, where she could hide under the duvet and think about the case... think about Amelia.

Maybe she was in way over her head after all.

CHAPTER TWENTY-FOUR

Mason made it back just in time to catch John Miller, the police department's best and brightest tech specialist. Only it looked as if he was leaving.

"Heading home?" Mason asked, jogging to catch up.

"Yep, finally," John replied, leading him down a maze of corridors as fast as his legs would carry him.

"I need you to do me a favor."

"Whatever it is, it will have to wait until morning."

Mason pulled the evidence bag from his pocket and slowed John to a stop, ignoring the instruction. "We might have some evidence on the Lullaby Killer here. Is it possible to recover it?"

John sighed, looked at the bag, and snatched it. He held it up to the light, glaring at the dirt that stained the inside of the bag. "Jeez, that looks like a real mess. Where'd you find this—the gutter?"

Mason just stared at him.

"Any water damage?"

"Not that I'm aware of."

John let out the same huff most techies use to announce their struggle with the science of technology. The bigger a fuss they made of it, the more they looked like heroes when they did their jobs right. "It might be. No guarantees. But like I say, you'll have to swing by in the morning." He handed back the bag and kept on walking, leaving Mason to catch up again.

"John, there's a killer out there. The quicker we sort this out, the better."

That was enough to make John stop and raise his voice, in spite of his smaller build compared to Mason's. "Uh, badge or not, you're still a civilian. So, I'm already doing you a big favor as it is. You want my help? You got it. But right now I'm heading home to be with my sick wife."

Mason watched him storm out and felt a dash of embarrassment. How was he supposed to have known that the guy's wife was sick? "Hey, I'm sorry about that. Truly, I am. But what the hell am I supposed to do in the meantime? Sit on my thumbs?"

"Go home," John shouted down the corridor without looking back. "Be with your own family."

Feeling helpless and irritated, Mason stuffed the evidence bag into his pocket and headed out front to where he'd left the car.

John obviously hadn't heard the latest.

CHAPTER TWENTY-FIVE

The car grumbled along the empty road. It was late, and Mason was trying not to disturb the neighborhood with the noisy engine. Besides, the fewer people who knew he was there, the better.

He stopped across the street and sat watching.

This is my home, for God's sake.

The lights were on inside, but only a vague silhouette could be seen behind the drapes. Mason pictured all the things that made him sick: Joshua hugging *his* daughter; going upstairs with *his* wife; making love to her in *his* bed.

It was enough to drive a man mad.

The silhouette moved, too, disappearing from behind one window and appearing at the next. A light soon flicked on in an upstairs room. Amy's room.

The drapes were open, and Mason could see her clearly. She was wearing her favorite scarlet sweater and examining the bookshelf with much contemplation. He couldn't see for sure at this distance, but he could picture her nose crinkling up like it usually did when she was concentrating. Amy finally decided on a book and sat in the window seat to dive into it.

Mason was so pleased that she'd turned out to be more of an academic type. If she'd been anything like her mother, she would be too vain to see outside of herself, and she definitely wouldn't lay her hands on a book—fiction or otherwise.

Mason wanted to knock. He longed to storm in and kick Joshua out, and then tell his wife that it was okay to put everything behind them and work things out. He was convinced all they needed was one tough conversation, and then they could strive toward a resolution.

No, he heard Evie saying somewhere in the recesses of his mind. *Keep your distance, sweet brother. No irrational moves.*

Who was he kidding anyway? Sandra would never go back now. Was Mason even sure he *wanted* to be back there? He was coming to understand his own feelings. It may not be that he even wanted his marriage back on the rails. More likely, he hated to have been betrayed by a goddamn Pilates instructor.

Sulking in self-pity, Mason finally called it a day. He started the engine and eased out of the spot, trying not to attract Amy's attention. Tonight, he would slip into the house without alerting Bill and Christine. Tomorrow...

Well, tomorrow was another day.

CHAPTER TWENTY-SIX

The killer had been awake all night, tossing, turning, and craving a kill.

For so long, he'd been keeping a low profile in San Francisco. Two years ago, when the detective had been snapping at his heels, he'd stayed away altogether. He'd even traveled long distances to continue his work. But now, he was back, working hard and desperate for more.

The sun was at last up, so he climbed out of bed and dressed in yesterday's clothes, got in the RV, and drove around the city. The roads were clear for this time of day, but he knew that would change as he got closer to the school.

He arrived within an hour and parked in sight of the front gates. The parents were just dropping their kids off and heading out to start their own days. The last of the buses were leaving, and the bell was about to ring, summoning kids to their classes.

But there were four who did not obey.

The Lullaby Killer watched them from the RV. One was a blonde girl with a face like a pissed-off supermodel and who clearly thought the world of herself. She was playing into the arms of a freckled redheaded boy, who was making sudden aggressive movements to scare the two children they had pinned against the wall. The bullied kids looked terrified, a boy and a girl, too similar in looks to only be friends. *Siblings?* mused the killer. *Twins, perhaps?*

Only one way to find out.

He climbed out of the RV and looked around, making sure he wasn't seen. When the coast was clear, he crossed the road and stormed toward the redheaded boy and his bitchy friend. "Get the hell away from my kids."

The expressions on the twins' faces—he could see now they were definitely twins—were amusing. It was confusion at first, blended with gratitude when they realized what was happening.

The blonde, going red in the face, spoke first. "They stole my money. They owe us."

"We didn't! I swear!" the twin boy protested.

"Liar!"

"All of you, shut up right now." The killer was under pressure. He needed a quick solution before he got caught here. He leaned over, put his hands on his knees, and beckoned the two bullies with his finger.

They inched closer.

"Get the fuck out of here," the killer whispered. "If I see you again, I'm going to break your stupid little legs." He pulled back his fist as if to throw a punch, which made them both jolt back before sprinting into the school without looking behind them.

"Whoa." The twins were laughing, their eyes wide.

"You're welcome," the Lullaby Killer said. "If I were you I'd stay away from those two."

"We can't help it," the girl told him. She looked smarter than the boy, which could become a problem at some stage. "We're in the same class."

"Yeah, we have to spend all day with them!" The boy seemed less with it, but still not stupid. Maybe he just led with his emotions too much, whether that was panic, fear, or excitement.

The killer could use that against him later.

"Why don't you take off?"

Their mouths hung open again.

"You mean leave school?" the girl asked. "Our dad would find out."

"I don't think so." The killer glanced around, itching to leave. "You'll be back before they know you've gone. Come on, let's go have some fun. Give me your hands."

They stood still for a long moment, looking at his outstretched palms and the gloves that covered them. They glanced at each other and then back at the killer.

Then they each took a hand.

The killer turned and led them toward the RV, confident it had all gone unnoticed.

This is going to be fun.

CHAPTER TWENTY-SEVEN

He'd parked under a bridge, away from the incoming drizzle, and, more importantly, away from human interaction. Nobody could disturb what he was about to do.

The back of the RV was a tin box made of steel he'd found on the scrap heap, and put together by a friend of a friend. The children didn't have to know it was soundproof, although they would've gotten a kick out of that.

"I've never had so much candy," said Ryan, the twin brother. "Not even at Christmas!"

"That's why Dad says not to have too much. You get all goofy like you are now." The girl, Kylie, rolled her eyes.

The killer sat under one of the four dim bulbs, snacking on the snowballs they'd picked up at the corner store an hour earlier.

Is this what they call grooming? He hoped not. He didn't want people to think he was having sex with children. The thought repulsed him, actually. All he wanted was to hurt them. The more tears, the better, but to actually touch them sexually repulsed him.

"I want to do something," Ryan said. "Can we do something? Can we play a game?"

The killer smiled a killer smile. "How about Truth or Dare?"

"That's a kid's game," Kylie said, as if she were any older than nine.

"Not the way I play it." The killer pulled out a bottle of vodka—a cheap bottle, but it would make no difference to them. "You tell a lie or don't perform the dare, you have to take a sip of this. It burns, but it will make you nice and drunk."

"I'm not touching that," Kylie said.

"Sheeeeeee's a chicken!" Ryan laughed while pointing.

The killer chuckled, too, knowing it might encourage her.

"Fine," she said. "Whatever." She folded her arms like a frustrated grump. "But I'll start. Truth or dare?"

The killer was on the spot, but he didn't mind. He would lie anyway, and they'd have no sure way of knowing. "Truth."

"Why do you wear those gloves?"

"I have bad skin," he lied, although the answer seemed to satisfy her. He turned to his right. "Ryan, truth or dare?"

"Truth!" He was far too giddy. It was hard to tell if he wanted the vodka or not.

"All right. Do you love your dad?"

"No!"

"Your sister?"

"Yuck!" He laughed. "No."

"That's not what you said in my birthday card," Kylie said, grinning at last.

The killer handed him the vodka, forcing back a smirk. "You know the rules."

Ryan took the bottle in both hands, judging how fast it might come out. It was like watching a puppy playing with a new toy. Ignoring Kylie's protests, he took a sip, spitting it out and coughing. "Disgusting!"

The killer took the bottle. "Yep, but it's for men, not boys."

"Your turn," Ryan gasped, turning to his sister. "Truth or—"

"Dare."

The boy was taken aback. "Okay, I dare you..." His eyes wandered around the back of the RV. "To take *two* sips of vodka! So either way, you lose, haha!"

In his mind, the killer praised the boy's intellect. He was smarter than his sister let him believe, and far cleverer than he'd first thought. It was probably Kylie's need to stand out from the crowd that gave the impression of more intelligence.

The killer would remember that when he crafted his next crime scene.

Making her decision, Kylie took the bottle and had only one sip before sliding it back to the middle, taking it easier than her brother had. "I want to go, now. I'm not comfortable with this."

"You'll go when I say you can go," the killer told her, forgetting his friendly smile. Recovering, he said, "I mean, we'll go soon. It's your turn, Kylie."

The fear in her eyes was not to be ignored. She hesitated, then said, "Truth or dare?"

"I'm going to take a dare this time." *So I won't have to lie to you, little girl.*

"I dare you to take us home."

"No, Kylie!" her brother shouted. "I don't want to go yet."

"It's okay, Ryan." The killer studied his options. Would he have to make his move now? He leaned forward, took the bottle, and downed a large gulp. It was easier than saying no, and the girl had trouble finding her voice. "Ryan, my man. Truth or dare?"

Light-headed from the vodka, the boy's eyes were roving all over the place. "Dare."

"I dare you to hit your sister."

"What? No!" Kylie got to her knees. "That's not fair."

"Ryan?" the killer demanded.

The boy crawled across the floor and gave a playful slap to the girl's arm, but it was still hard enough for her to wince. He shuffled back to his corner of the RV.

"Come on, boy. A little harder."

"We won't—"

"Shut up right now!" the killer yelled at her, losing his patience with the little brat. "Ryan, give her a real punch, will ya?"

Kylie was shaking as her brother approached her. She must have understood the threat of the situation a little more than he did, and that worked in his favor. His knuckles clunked across her skull with a beautiful thumping sound.

Kylie held her head. A tear brewed in her eye as she complained. "Please, take us home now. I don't want to be here."

The killer appraised the tears filling her eyes above reddening cheeks. "Tell you what—one more go and I'll drive you back to school. But this time, I want to ask you, Kylie... truth or dare?"

The girl was taking care with her answer. Considering the whack she'd just taken from her brother, it seemed that a simple question might be safer for the both of them. She sniffed, held her head with pride, and said, "Truth."

Shuffling forward, the killer leaned in close to her face and ground his teeth. "Are you getting out of here alive?"

Kylie sobbed while Ryan sat chuckling to himself, the alcohol already taking its effect. She cleared her throat as her lip quivered and a tear rolled down her cheek. "Yes."

Satisfied with the response, the killer sat back as a smile broke out across his face—a genuine one this time. With his gloved right hand, he poked the bottle her way, scraping it across the metal floor of the RV. "Drink."

CHAPTER TWENTY-EIGHT

It was early morning when Mason slipped out of the house, careful to avoid Bill and Christine. He didn't want to have to explain himself, so he headed straight for the station and directly to the tech lab.

Inside was buzzing with technicians both young and old whizzing around their computers or testing something on what looked like a miniature target range.

But John was nowhere to be found.

"He's late today. Should be here any minute," said a helpful young woman.

John soon arrived and dumped his satchel onto the desk, looking at Mason with frustration. He was pushing his luck. "Hand me the damn phone, will you?"

Mason wanted to scream at the guy for his attitude, but for as long as he needed something from him he would have to play it safe. Then again...

"Just do your job, and I won't have to send Detective Harvey down here to give you an earful."

John shot him a look of angry submission, then snatched the phone and ran it under a microscope. It was a laborious process that stiffened Mason's back over the course of several hours, but eventually they had something of a result.

"Okay, the memory card is a broken piece of junk, so hopefully any data was saved to the phone itself." He placed it on the desk between them and turned it on with latex-gloved hands. "What are you hoping to find on here?" he asked as it was loading up.

Mason couldn't tell if he was genuinely curious of if he was just making an awkward scene more comfortable, but he graced him with an answer nonetheless. "Anything that might give an ID of the killer."

The screen lit up, and John scrolled to the gallery. "She's all yours."

"Thanks." Mason held it with both hands, careful not to dislodge the broken pieces. He scanned through the photos, finding a couple of dark and blurry images. The timestamp said they were taken around the right time on the day of the murder. Feeling hopeful, Mason located the video folder.

He was horrified by what he found.

While the video was dark and blurry, all sound muffled by the ambience of heavy rainfall, there was the unmistakable groan of a van door sliding closed. The camera was all over the place, until it focused on the silhouette of a man. He had a baseball cap on, and it was tough to make out his face.

"It's not enough," Mason whispered to himself.

"What?"

"Shh."

Listening closely to nothing more than the thrumming of rain and Sampson's heavy breathing, Mason hoped for a clue. When the boy came into view, Mason felt his heart clench at the thought of little Thomas Chance and the horrific way he'd been tortured before his murder.

What kind of sick bastard does this?

And then the camera moved.

The cameraman was climbing out of his car, swooping around an enormous RV.

"Is the RV of use to you?" John asked.

"No. There are literally thousands just like that one around the city. Even my aunt had one."

But then his luck changed. The camera was pointed directly at the license plate of the RV before Sampson stepped back to allow the whole vehicle into the camera's view. *Smart kid*, Mason thought, to have gotten all this information on record.

"It seems too suspicious," James Sampson said on the video.

Mason pressed his ear to the phone when he heard the voice.

"I'm going to follow them."

Then the video stopped. The recordings and pictures ended there, but at least something useful had come from them.

"Seems informative," John said.

"Yeah." Mason was thrilled to have something work

out okay for once, and through all the excitement of catching up to the killer he barely noticed his current heartache. "Send that to my phone, will you? And a screenshot of the man." It was blurry, but it was better than nothing. At least now he had the license plate number to an RV.

He just had to find its owner.

CHAPTER TWENTY-NINE

The RV was registered to a Mr. Frank Marley but had been reported as stolen a few weeks ago. As Marley lived outside the city, Mason took his number from the registration and called to make sure he'd be home. More than anything, Marley seemed grateful his vehicle had been found. Mason would have to break it to him that it hadn't actually been recovered.

It took a couple of hours to reach him, and he was greeted at the door of a large and well-kept house by a man who looked like he was the good model in a dentistry commercial.

Mason introduced himself and was shown into a room, which was even more impressive than the exterior. Sandalwood beams reached across the high ceiling, propped up by beautiful red pillars. Everything tiled was white and shiny. It was a posterworthy home.

"I'm sorry to have to tell you, but your vehicle is not within our possession," Mason told him, noticing the man's frown. "Have you ever heard of the Lullaby Killer?"

"Of course," Frank said. "Wait... I knew I'd seen you somewhere before! You're the PI working the case, right?" He was smiling now, his eyes alight as if he'd met a celebrity and was suddenly starstruck.

"How did you know?"

"I read your sister's blog all the time. Fascinating stuff, man! You're like that detective from the TV! Hey, listen, if there's any way I can help you, just tell me how."

Mason had no idea he was known outside of his own working circle. Evie must have been doing better than she'd let on. He felt his face heat to a deep red. "As a matter of fact, that's what I'm here for. We think it was the killer who stole your RV. Did you see anything suspicious around the time it was taken?"

Frank showed Mason to the couch and sat with him. "I had, sure. I was being followed for a couple of weeks before it went missing by a weird-looking guy who appeared everywhere I turned. At first I thought it was just coincidence."

"I see," Mason said, flicking through his cell phone. He found the picture of the man and held it out. "Is this the man you saw?"

Frank squinted. "It's hard to say. But he *was* wearing a baseball cap, just like this guy. And the gloves, too."

"Gloves?" Mason recalled Susan Chance saying the same thing.

"I remember because it was summertime. His hands must have been roasting in those things." His eyes darkened with horrific realization. "Oh shit, do you think he'll come back to kill me?"

"I sincerely doubt that, Mr. Marley." Mason's cell phone rang, vibrating in his hand. It was Bill, and his timing was bad as usual. He put the phone to one side, balancing it on the armrest of the couch. "And nothing else came of it? No threats? No freak occurrences?"

Frank shook his head. "Not really. A couple crank calls, but that could have been anyone. Hey, why do you think he chose to steal from me?"

The cell phone rang—Bill again.

"You live outside the city. Other than that, I'd say it's random. Mind if I take this?"

"Go ahead." Frank left to give Mason privacy. He was a curious guy, eccentric and humble, yet inquisitive and excited. Shaking off the oddity of the man, Mason answered the phone. "Hello?"

"Hey, buddy," Bill said. "Listen, I need you to run an errand for me."

"I'm kind of busy right now."

"No, this will benefit you, believe me. Two kids have gone missing from Pickerage School. Nine-year-old twins."

"That's the same school Daniels and Chance attended." Mason's mouth went bone-dry with anticipation. *Has the killer really been sticking to a pattern?*

"Exactly. The police can't do anything for another day or so. Not officially. But an outside party should have no trouble. Want to have a word with the father?"

This was exactly the kind of information he'd been

hoping to get. "Text me the address, will you? I'll swing by shortly."

"Will do."

Mason thanked Frank for his time and left his card in case he remembered something. He barely realized he was running to his Mustang as he hopped in and tore down the road toward the home of the missing twins.

CHAPTER THIRTY

Nothing could have stopped Evie from checking in on her.

As soon as she'd seen her crossing the street, she'd followed as closely as possible. On numerous occasions she nearly lost her, so she picked up her speed to catch up.

When Amelia headed into the mall, Evie parked the car, went to the ground floor, and worked her way up. After a long and arduous search, she finally spotted her in the clothing department of a store, trying on shoes with a friend. Amelia had no idea what Evie looked like, so she was free to move around as much as she liked.

It was wonderful to see her again, as heartbreaking as it was. She wondered about the email and whether the sender had actually known where Amelia lived. *He couldn't, could he? And who is this anonymous emailer? The killer?* Evie could dig around without difficulty, but she knew it came with a risk of putting the girl in danger.

Amelia left with her purchases and headed toward the food court, where she took a seat at the center table. This made it a lot easier for Evie to keep an eye on her from the railing on the floor above.

From out of nowhere, a nightmarish thought occurred to her.

Is the killer here now, watching us?

Evie looked all around. Everything seemed perfectly normal, but the killer had blended in for over three years, so he was damn good at staying discreet. Farther along the railing, one man stood looking down at the food court. It was tough to discern whether he was looking at Amelia or not. But when a woman crept up behind and showered him with kisses, Evie understood that the only thing he'd killed was time.

The phone rang in her pocket, snatching her attention.

"Yep."

"Evie, it's Mason. Where are you?"

"Just, you know, hanging around."

"Well, head over to Southwell Terrace. There's been a development."

Evie had no idea how to say this, so she just blurted it. "I'm out."

There was a pause on Mason's end. Then, "What?"

"Yeah, I was thinking about it. I don't think I have the energy to pursue this thing. But you don't have to worry, I won't publish any more news about it."

"What the hell, Evie? You were hot for this case only yesterday."

He sounded more pissed off than she'd ever heard him before, and she felt awful for letting him down like this. After all, she was his supporting shoulder throughout this difficult time in his life.

"I'm sorry, I just can't do it."

Downstairs, Amelia got up from her seat. Evie's heart thumped until she saw that she was only going to the bathroom. "How are *you* doing, anyway? Have you heard any more from Sandra?"

"No. Enough of the small talk already. Are you in or not?"

"I'm..." It was impossible to help Mason find the killer *and* protect Amelia. The choice was never going to be easy. "I'm not."

Mason sighed. "Fine," he said, before the line went dead.

What am I supposed *to do?*

CHAPTER THIRTY-ONE

Mason hung up the phone and continued driving toward the twins' house. He trawled through his memory, clawing away at the darkest corners to remember lullabies that included twins. Nothing sprang to mind.

He arrived at a huge and expensive-looking house that reminded him of his own home—or what had been his home, up until recently. Mason strode up the pathway and was met by a distraught man with obvious pain in his sunken brown eyes.

"I was led to understand Detective Harvey would make an appearance," he said, looking at Mason with understandable suspicion.

"The police have rules, sir, and can't get to you for another day or so. But Bill is a good friend of mine, and I assure you I'll do everything I can."

Although reluctant, the man introduced himself as Owen Carter and let Mason in. He zipped around the kitchen, hastily cleaning up. "I don't know what to do with myself. I'm stir-crazy, you know?"

Mason could see exactly what he meant. It wasn't uncommon to fidget when you were expecting bad news. "So, about the twins..."

"Detective Harvey said something about this Lullaby Killer I've been seeing in the news. Do you think it's him? Do you think he's responsible?"

"It's hard to say at this point," Mason explained. "It certainly follows the pattern, but we shouldn't jump to any conclusions. For all we know, they just decided to run away from home for a while."

"They just wouldn't do that. They're happy children. They... Do you think they're alive, Mr. Black?" He looked as if he only wanted one answer, but Mason didn't like to bullshit people if he could help it.

"I think they are at the moment, yes. But in these kinds of situations, we have to act fast. I take it you've not had any kind of note, or a ransom? Nothing like that?"

"No." The man's eyes widened. "Should I expect one?"

"I wouldn't rule it out, but we don't want to depend on it. If this is who we think it is, we don't have long to act. The first thing I need you to do is start an appeal. Do you use social media? Facebook? Twitter?"

"I... Yeah, I use Twitter." Owen finally stopped shuffling around.

"Good. Get a picture out as soon as possible. If either of your kids passes someone in the street, we've got to increase the chances of that person recognizing them. Got it?"

Owen went straight for his laptop, not wasting a second. It was obvious he just wanted his pain to end. To his right sat a framed picture of two kids—a boy and a girl of equal age.

"Is that them?"

Owen glanced over and nodded.

Mason picked up the frame and aimed his cell phone directly at the photo, taking a snapshot of his own. The girl especially caught his eye—she looked a little like Amy, only younger and with mouse-brown hair.

"Done," Owen said. "What happens next?"

"Next, contact every blogger and independent press agent you can. Newspapers take too long, so stay local and get your plea viral. If we can get the abductor to realize you have money, there might be chance of a ransom—if there isn't already."

"Got it," the man said, his voice croaky. He stood, staring at Mason. "I'm going to have a drink. Would you like one?"

"If it's Jack or stronger, sure."

While the man splashed alcohol into a couple of tumblers, Mason went on.

"I'm going to do everything I can to get your kids back. I assure you. Meanwhile..." He took the Jack and sipped it, the droolworthy scent lifting his senses. "Thanks. Meanwhile, keep up all the presswork. Here's my card, should you need it."

"Thank you, Mr. Black. Do you have kids?"

"I have a girl. She's thirteen."

Owen sipped his drink. "Be sure to take care of her. You'll never realize just how much you love her until something happens."

But Mason didn't want to think about Amy right now. He needed to stay sharp, alcohol buzz and all. "Anyway, I'll be in touch. You've got my number. Let me know if you hear anything."

Mason downed his drink and left the Carters' house with no expectation of anything, other than finding two more dead bodies accompanied by a gruesome message.

CHAPTER THIRTY-TWO

"This is where you're going to die."

The children trembled on the shadowy sands beneath the Golden Gate Bridge, with dusk setting in and icy roars blasting at their skin from across the bay. Even the Lullaby Killer was freezing his rocks off. He would have to make this quick.

He continued to dig, both frightened and excited at the possibility of getting caught with these kids. The last time had been such an intrusive interruption, but the payoff had been something sweet. He could still hear the *thunk* of the hammer as it crushed the man's skull.

"What are... th-those for?" Ryan asked, pointing at the heavy craft scissors.

It was surprising to hear him speak up for once. It seemed he finally understood the danger of this scenario.

"Hehe." The killer crooked his pinkie finger, then carried on scooping shovel-loads of sand across the beach.

Golden slumbers kiss your eyes, he thought. This one would be particularly special.

"You're going to kill us, aren't you?" little Kylie asked, trying to disguise her fear. It wasn't working. "Is that your plan?"

Once again, the killer stopped digging, staring at her until he at last shook his head no. It was fun to see the relief in the twins' eyes. They probably hoped to be home safe by this time tomorrow. He would put a stop to that. "See, all I'm going to do is bury you to your necks. It's the tide that's gonna kill you."

The twins shook in fear, clutching each other's hands as the killer howled with laughter. Although darkness was fast approaching, he could still make out their bloodshot eyes before he finished digging the first of the two holes.

"Our dad'll kill you," Kylie said, weeping. "He'll find you and kill you."

The killer uttered a callous chuckle and started on the second hole. "And how's he gonna manage that? San Francisco's finest have been looking for me for years. This is my city, little girl. Nobody can get in the way of my fun."

"But he's got money. He can hire anyone he needs to find you." The girl sniffed as her brother squeezed her hand tighter.

Wait.

The killer paused.

No. No, no. He continued with the last of the sand,

but with less enthusiasm than before. He couldn't, could he? *It ain't about money,* he told himself. *It's about curing America's problem. But if I had the money...*

"How much?"

Kylie wiped her eyes with her sleeve. "What?"

"How much money's he got?"

She shrugged. "A lot, I guess. We have maids."

The killer didn't want to believe it, but they did seem to have been of a higher class than his usual choice. Sure, they attended a public school, but they spoke correctly and their posture was far too proper for normal kids of their age. But he couldn't risk it. "Don't make no difference."

He raised the shovel and dug it deep into the sand. As he drove his foot onto it for more pressure, the girl must have seen her opportunity—or was consumed by desperation.

She leapt from where she'd been sitting, clawing at the sand as she scrambled to her feet and blazed up the shore into the distance, screaming in high-pitched wails.

If anyone heard them, it would all be over.

"Get back here!" The killer took off after her, pausing only briefly to tell Ryan he'd gut him if he moved. He hadn't run like this in a long time but was still fast enough to gain some distance before they reached the rundown neighborhood.

Kylie dived out of sight behind a small white-paneled church. The killer had to stop. If he went any farther, he risked the boy running off, too. Turning, he could see him in the distance. Maybe he could head off just a little, but...

But then you'd lose them both, stupid.

"Fuck! Shit!" he yelled, then marched back toward Ryan and the two empty graves.

CHAPTER THIRTY-THREE

It was something Mr. Carter had said about his daughter: *You be sure to take care of her.*

And how could he not? Paying no mind to the incoming calls from Bill, Mason sped the Mustang toward his house. Even if he couldn't patch things up completely with Sandra, there was still hope he could repair some bridges.

What about Joshua? queried the voice in his head as he shifted into fifth. It was as though a ten-ton block was tied to his heart. Could he really forgive her? Even if he tried his damndest, could he really remove the image of somebody else touching his wife with such intimacy? Every second he spent wondering convinced him he could not.

But he had to try.

When he arrived, the front door was open and Sandra was leaving. Mason left his car and went to her, just as she was about to open her own car door.

"What are you doing here?" she asked, her teeth grinding.

"I just wanted to talk." Mason raised his hands in mock surrender.

"Well, now's not a good time. I have to collect Amy from school." Sandra opened the door and threw in her purse. She was about to climb in when Mason held the door open.

"How about after? We could go somewhere for dinner. My treat."

"Joshua's taking us out." Sandra got in the car.

He could see it now: the straightened black hair, the polished nails, the not-too-revealing top, which was just provocative enough to be suggestive. "Right, Joshua."

"Excuse me." Sandra tried to pull the door shut, but he held it firmly.

"He's back," Mason blurted, but he was no longer talking about Joshua. He waited for a reaction while Sandra sat staring through the windshield. He knew that look—she was assessing her options.

And then she stared up at him.

"You're sure?"

Mason nodded. "I want you to take extra care around Amy, you hear? Whatever feud exists between you and me, don't forget about her safety."

Sandra rolled her eyes. "I know how to take care of my daughter."

Our daughter, Mason thought, but saying it aloud would only raise a rattlesnake.

"I have to go." Sandra tried once more to close the door.

"Where did we go wrong?" Mason hated to put himself out there so desperately, but everything had happened so fast. Even if she'd doubted their marriage for years, surely it'd been her responsibility to tell him. Now, here he was, begging for some kind of explanation while his wife ran into the arms of some other guy.

"*You* went wrong the moment you put your work before your family."

"That was two years ago. I left the force for you. In the middle of a case, no less."

"And now what're you doing with your time?"

It stung enough that he let go of the door and watched her pull out of the drive. Mason simply could not understand what he'd done wrong. Sure, he could admit to putting in too much overtime at the office, but was it not for a good cause? Or had she been looking for a reason to move on to someone new anyway?

For the next hour he sat in his car, ignoring further calls from Bill and thinking of the woman he'd just spoken to, who now seemed nothing more than a stranger.

Can't you see I was trying to do some good? To catch a killer?

Fueled by a confusing mix of hurt and anger, he slid the keys in the ignition and the car roared to life. At least he could head to Bill's house now, lock himself in the spare bedroom, and welcome nurture from a bottle of something strong.

CHAPTER THIRTY-FOUR

The press swarmed him as he arrived at Bill's house. All over the drive and across the lawn, reporters surrounded his car like hungry puppies begging to their master. Mason could barely get out of the car, and when he did, the same problem kept him from the front door.

"Mr. Black, is it true the Lullaby Killer is back?"

"Are you working with the police?"

"Have you exchanged words with Mr. Carter?"

The noise was unbearable. The last thing Mason needed now was his face all over the media. Was this a backlash of having Owen make press statements? Had his name been dropped without his knowledge?

Mason finally reached the door and had to squeeze through, covering his face to prevent more photos of him. The more he was exposed, the more danger he'd put his family in.

"Where the hell have you been?" Bill was inside, storming toward him with a phone in his hand and Christine awkwardly smiling behind him. "I've been trying to call you."

Mason knew that tone. "What's happened?"

"Those missing twins? One of them was found running down Elmgrove. She was struck by a car, but she's okay."

He should have been overjoyed that one of them had been recovered, but that was just it... "Only one of them?"

"The daughter, Kylie. She was screaming her head off, something about how her brother was being buried under the Golden Gate Bridge."

"Have you had it searched?"

"Every square inch, but nothing's turned up. The killer probably hightailed it out of there as soon as the girl got away."

Mason rubbed his palms over his eyes and took a deep breath. Was the boy dead, or had he gotten away, too? "All right. So where's the girl now?"

Bill grabbed his coat from the hook and slid his arms inside. "At the hospital. Come on, we'll take your car." He turned to Christine. "I'm sorry you have to put up with the cameras, honey. Just keep the doors and blinds closed. Call me if you need anything."

Mason opened the door, and they headed for the car, battling through another assault of unanswerable questions. They got in and dashed to the hospital, where Kylie

Carter lay unconscious. Mason felt like a monster for having to extract information from her, but if she was able to talk, he'd need to hear everything she had to say.

CHAPTER THIRTY-FIVE

Evie had drawn the drapes and not seen a shred of daylight since. With a pillow as her cuddle companion, she had no further reason to leave the couch. Even her laptop remained in the corner, unused.

The news was playing on the TV—something about a false Val Salinger sighting in Paris—but she paid it no mind. Instead, she continued to stare at an open book, the page unturned in a long time.

All she could think about was Mason, and how she'd let him down. Evie tried to convince herself she wouldn't have been much use to him anyway, but she knew it was far from the truth. Without her counsel he would go off the rails, like he had before he'd met Sandra—a rapid downward spiral into alcoholism.

The news report moved on to the next story, and Evie's ears pricked up. It was the voice of her brother, saying "no comment" as he shoved through a crowd of journalists. Watching them now, she cringed at the idea she used to be one of them.

Such insensitive pricks.

Mason looked different, there was no denying that. He looked scruffier, his skin paler and his cheeks unshaven. The darkening bags under his eyes spoke volumes.

Evie wanted to help him, but what about Amelia? She just couldn't risk letting any harm come to her. So, what else was there to do?

Well, she thought, *there is one thing...*

It was a bad idea. A terrible idea, really. She'd be breaking the law. But if it was for a good cause, perhaps she could justify it. If it would allow her to continue providing information to her brother, and vice versa, then why shouldn't she do it? Besides, there would be no written proof—it was more of a verbal arrangement.

Evie sat upright, sniffed her armpits, and tugged on her hair. She then threw on something warm and grabbed her keys. It was an exhilarating feeling, like the one you get when you're spending money on something you know you can't afford.

Stumbling in the dark, she quickly opened her laptop and confirmed the address hadn't changed, then headed for the door with her nerves in tatters.

I can't believe I'm doing this after all these years.

CHAPTER THIRTY-SIX

They soon arrived at the hospital to meet a relieved but distressed Owen Carter.

"How are you, sir?" Mason asked, noting the red-raw eyes.

"I don't know what to think. I'm so pleased to see Kylie again, but I can't stop thinking about where Ryan is."

"How is she?" Bill asked as they moved from the waiting room into the corridor.

"A few bumps and scratches. She woke up a half hour ago. I told her you were coming."

Mason felt useless. He kept walking with his head up and his hands buried in the pockets of his trench coat.

When they reached the door, Owen lowered his voice. "Please don't put too much of a strain on her. She's as scared as I am."

"Just relax. She's going to be fine." Mason entered the room, shutting Bill and the girl's father out. The truth was, he was just as concerned about what he might hear.

Inside, a machine was beeping and a girl lay prone in a bed across the room. Her skin was bruised like a peach, her appearance nothing like her picture now. A cast covered her arm, and a lost expression adorned her face.

"Kylie, my name's Mason Black. I'm the lead investigator assigned to your case."

The girl looked at him and blinked big hazel eyes. "It's nice to meet you."

Mason realized he was staring. He snapped himself from his trance and pulled a chair over beside her bed. "I'm here to ask you some questions. You don't have to answer them all, but the more you tell me, the better chance I have of finding your brother."

The girl nodded and winced. The car must have hit her at quite a speed.

He took the cell phone from his pocket and showed her the photo from the National Park. "Is this the man who abducted you?"

Kylie squinted her eyes at the dark and blurry picture. "I think so."

"Great. And did you happen to see any distinguishing features? A tattoo, a scar, anything like that?" Mason already felt he was putting too much on her. But she was a brave girl, and it seemed she could handle it.

Kylie thought for a moment. "No. Oh, but he wore gloves the whole time."

There it was again. What was it about the gloves? "The *whole* time?"

"Yes, sir," she said, her voice weak. "Even in the RV, which was pretty warm."

Mason was just about to ask that question. Knowing this was how he'd been taking the children, his chances of finding the killer had improved. It seemed they only had to find the RV, and they would find their guy. "Can you describe the contents of the RV? Did he have any possessions or framed photographs that stood out? Files? Books?"

"No, nothing like that. It was... metal."

"Metal?"

The girl licked her lips. "It was like a metal box in the back. The walls, the floor. Everything."

"Like a box?"

"Yes." A tear rolled down the girl's cheek and hit her pillow. "The man was so angry when I ran. Before that, he just seemed happy, I guess."

Mason was confused. "Excuse me, you said he seemed *happy*?"

"No," she said. "I mean, when I mentioned money he wanted to listen. I think."

Although it sent a chill through Mason, maybe this was a good thing. Now he knew the boy's father was wealthy, their chances of receiving a ransom note had raised considerably.

"Mr. Black, will my brother be okay?"

Mason didn't want to lie, but he could hardly tell her the truth. "I'm doing everything I can." The truth of it was, he had no idea. "Thank you for your time, Kylie. I have to go and do some work. I'll send your father in."

"Be careful," she called after him as he went for the door. "The bad man hates you."

Perspiration brewed under his collar, heat searing his skin as if from nowhere. Mason stopped dead in his tracks. "He talked about me?"

The girl nodded. "He told me you were looking for him, and that you're his biggest problem."

He stood staring at the floor. It felt different now he'd been acknowledged. Mason imagined the killer targeting Amy, and he sighed. "You got that right."

Outside the room, Bill was along the corridor on the phone. He spotted Mason and jogged toward him, hanging up. "How fast can you get to Southside Bay?"

"Why, what's up?"

"We put out a notice about that RV of yours, and a civilian just called in. Says she just saw it outside her home."

Mason's heart thundered in his chest, and he picked up speed. "On my way."

CHAPTER THIRTY-SEVEN

Usually, calls from a neighborhood like this came from some bored, attention-seeking housewives or desperate teenagers, anyone who thought they could turn heads by claiming they saw something they didn't.

In this case it was a single mother.

The woman who came to the door was a mess: greasy hair matted to her face, stained sweatpants, and too much cheap perfume. Mason empathized with the blue-eyed toddler in her arms.

"Yeah, I seen it," she said with pride. "A big ol' thing that parks here every Friday after school. My kids don't like it too much. They say he creeps 'em out."

"They've seen the owner?" Mason adjusted his stance in the cool air, wishing she'd invite him in. At least the rain had taken a brief break.

"Sure. One day, I was doing my laundry, and my boy Judas came running in screaming like crazy. Said the man whistled him over and asked him to get in, said he'd take him to a place called Mayfairer."

"What's Mayfairer?"

"I ain't got no idea. Could be a cemetery for all I know."

Mason tried to think of any cemetery-based lullabies. *Nothing.* "Did you see him?"

"Yeah, I seen him. Got that creep's picture, too."

"You got his *picture*?" This seemed far too good to be true. "Would you mind if I take a look?"

The woman looked as if she'd been asked to perform a miracle. "Hold on."

While she was gone, Mason stepped back and took a glance at the house. It was a tacky place, stickers on the windows and dog shit on the lawn, though he hadn't seen or heard a dog while he'd been standing at the door.

The woman returned and handed him a photo printed on a sheet of paper. "Took it with my cell phone and printed it ma-self. You can keep that."

Mason's hands shook as he examined the photo. *Is this the guy?* he wondered. *Is this the guy who's given the San Francisco Police so much trouble? The one who's given* me *so much grief?* He'd expected someone bigger and older. Maybe someone more intelligent or devious-looking. But this man was small, younger, and looked kind of harmless.

"Thing is," the woman went on, "I seen him a few times before, too. Seemed to be wherever I went, I'd turn around and see that damn RV. One day, I even mustered the courage to go and bang on his door, fixing to give him a piece of my mind for following me, but... there wasn't nobody there. So, I waited to follow him, ya know? Make sure he wasn't up to no good."

"I see. Good thinking. And what did you find?" Mason encouraged her to speed up her storytelling. *Kylie Carter spoke with more clarity than this woman, for God's sake.*

"Well, he ended up at Rigby's," she said, like it was supposed to mean something.

"Rigby's?"

"Uh-huh. Trailer park up the road. It's where all good trailers go to die."

Mason snorted a laugh. "Can you point me in the right direction?"

The woman scribbled a messy but readable map on the back of his business card and Mason followed the directions as best he could, excited that he might just get lucky and find a trace of the RV.

CHAPTER THIRTY-EIGHT

Evie had never been so nervous. The house was bigger and better than she remembered it, meaning only that she'd made the right choice all those years ago. She was mentally preparing herself, summoning the nerve to knock on the door.

What the hell was I thinking?

A sudden question of conscience made her turn on her heels and walk away without knocking. She'd made it down three steps before the door clicked open.

"May I help you?"

Evie turned to the voice. It was Mary, the owner of the house and the person she wanted to speak to. She was slightly older than Evie, midforties and a real Oprah type. If Oprah was white, that was.

"I'm sorry."

Mary's mouth hung open as she squinted her eyes. "Evelyn? Is that you?" She didn't look pleased to see her, but why would she? "You shouldn't be here."

"I know, but it's important. Can I come in?"

For a moment Mary just stared, looking alarmed. Then she pulled the door open wider and stepped back. "You'd better make this quick. I'm a busy woman."

"Thank you." Evie stepped into the house, where everything was cream-colored and polished. "You've had a lot of work done."

"It *has* been thirteen years." Mary showed her to the couch. "You said this was important. Is it something I did, or something I can do?"

"It's neither." Evie spotted a picture frame but tried not to look at the happy family. "Have you heard about the Lullaby Killer?"

"From the news? Some psycho snatching up children, right?" Mary clasped her hands and couldn't keep them still. It was a clear-cut sign of discomfort.

"Yes. Well, he has a problem with me."

Mary sat forward. "And you're here because...?"

"Because he mentioned Amelia."

Silence descended around the room. Both women gazed at each other.

"I think you should leave," Mary said, standing up.

Evie rose with her. "Look, you don't have to like it, but you need to go somewhere. Take Amelia with you until all of this has blown over. Do you have somewhere you can go?"

Mary looked insulted. "Well, yes, but I don't see why we sho—"

"If you give a damn about Amelia, there's *every* reason why you should."

"Excuse me? Don't you come into my house and threaten her. She became *my* daughter as soon as you signed the papers. You have no right to come back here now and start acting like a concerned mother."

"It's not a threat, Mary. I just—"

"Get out. Get out right now, or—"

The front door swung open and a high-spirited teenage girl came tearing through the room. "Hey, Mom," she said, kissing Mary on the cheek. She stopped and looked at Evie, pausing as if she recognized a part of herself in her features.

"Amelia, this is my... my friend, Evelyn."

Evie's heart raced inside her chest. She'd seen Amelia from a distance but never imagined she would ever get to speak with her. She wasn't even sure if she'd wanted to, until now. "Nice to meet you."

"Nice to meet you, too," Amelia said, shaking Evie's hand. "Are you staying for dinner?"

"Evelyn has to go," Mary intruded.

"Oh, okay. Well, I have homework to do. Nice to meet you, Evelyn." Amelia took off, heading upstairs to do what most thirteen-year-olds refused to do at all costs.

Evie stood, shocked.

"Please leave. Now. You shouldn't have come here." Mary took her by the arm and showed her to the door with more urgency than she should have.

"Wait. Will you take her someplace or not? I need to know."

Mary opened the door and paused, clenching her jaw. Then, "Fine."

"Thank you." Evie breathed a sigh of relief and stepped out onto the porch.

"Don't set foot on my property again. Ever." Mary slammed the door, leaving Evie alone in the cold with her heart melted and her head a jumble of thoughts.

At least Amelia would be safe.

CHAPTER THIRTY-NINE

The Lullaby Killer's phone pinged before it lit up the dark.

Another email alert from the news site: the father of the twins wanted to make a statement. The killer touched the link and opened the video, which showed a man with red eyes and a solemn glare. He had the police behind him and a mass of reporters begging for information at his feet.

How pathetic.

"It's with great relief that I can announce the safe return of my daughter, Kylie," he read from the cue card. *"Although she was able to get away, she was struck down by a driver as she ran for safety. We will not be pressing charges."*

The killer skipped the video on. He didn't care for gratitude or well-being. He was still pissed off that the girl had tried to run from him, and even more aggravated that she'd succeeded. But now he cared for one only thing —how desperate the man was to see his son alive.

"And I pray that my son is returned to me. If anyone has any details that may help the investigation, please contact..." The video went on, but the drama ended there. Perhaps it was time for the killer to send in his ransom. But how much should he ask for? One hundred thousand? Two? Most people would pay anything for their children's safety.

"Is that my dad?" The voice behind him was weak and whiny.

"Does it matter? It all ends the same for you."

Little Ryan Carter whimpered in the corner, his arms folded and his face buried into them.

"Quit your crying, boy." The killer set down his cell phone and continued to tap away at the keyboard. There was a lot to get done, but he couldn't do it with that sobbing noise behind him, ruining his focus.

"Please, just let me go."

"I said shut it!" The killer turned and pointed a finger, bellowing at the kid. "Little boys should be seen but not heard, and you're pissing me off."

"I just want to go home and—"

The killer shot to his feet, grabbing the nearby scissors. "Back at the beach, you asked me what these are for." He stepped forward, leaning toward Ryan and spitting through his teeth. "Another word out of you and I'll show you."

His anger getting the best of him, the killer launched the scissors across the room, smashing through something made of glass. Distracted by his jittering nerves, he dropped back into his chair and continued his work. *Damn kid's more trouble than he's worth.* But how much was he worth?

It was time to find out.

CHAPTER FORTY

Mason headed into Rigby's trailer park with the plate number and a better photograph. He clutched them tight, unwilling to lose the progress he'd made. And with the dark gray clouds crawling all over San Francisco, he feared they might get wet.

The ground was mostly dirt that squelched under Mason's boots as he trudged through the site. The woman had been right; it was where all good trailers came to die.

All around him were row after row of battle-scarred trailers, some of which had once given less-fortunate families a place to live. There was no getting past it, of course; 90 percent of the people who lived in these things were junkies or fugitives.

Screwing up his nose at the lingering mustiness, Mason headed for the reception booth, where an underweight and grubby-faced teenager sat fiddling with a chunk of metal. He looked up as though he hadn't seen another human being in years.

"Mason Black, private investigator. I'm looking for an RV." He took out the plate number and held it up to the glass.

The boy—no older than sixteen—got to his feet and came around to a nearby door, meeting with Mason face-to-face. "Yeah, it comes by here a lot. Hey, man, can I interest you in some spares? We got bits for all sorts of things. Check this out." He leaned into the booth once again and pulled out a VCR. "Still in good working order, look. Even cleaned it and tested my *Tom & Jerry* tapes. Reckon it's worth a fortune, but you can have it for…" He looked to be calculating a large sum in his head. "Eighty bucks."

Mason stood in shock and tried to stifle a laugh. He couldn't even remember the last time he'd seen a VCR. "Just the RV today, kid."

The boy lowered his head. "Oh, sure. Okay." He went back inside the booth and pulled a hardbound book from an overhead shelf, flicked it open, and perused the vehicle log. "Yeah, thought so. It's every two weeks, and he comes and parks in lot B. It's out back."

"How long does he stay for? Does he say what he wants?"

"A couple days or so. Usually takes some scrap metal and throws it in the RV."

Mason nodded and showed the photograph. "Is this him?"

The kid leaned forward and nodded. "Yeah, man, that's him for sure. Is he under arrest?"

"I'm just a PI, kid, with as much power to arrest

someone as you. I just want to ask him some questions." Mason played it down for a reason. If he made a big deal about the fact he was tracking a serial killer, the boy might let an early warning slip. Then it would all be over. "Do me a favor? Here's my card." He slid it into the payment tray. "Give me a call next time he comes by here."

The kid took the card and looked it over with intrigue. "Sure. Except I won't need to call ya. He's here right now."

CHAPTER FORTY-ONE

Mason stormed toward the Mustang and grabbed his revolver from the glove compartment. He considered calling for backup—or even just calling Bill—but people were encouraged to be absolutely certain they needed help before rounding up the cavalry.

The boy ran behind him, struggling to keep up. "Slow down, mister!"

But Mason had no reason to stop. For all he knew, the Lullaby Killer was just around the corner and could even be caught in the act. He imagined finding Ryan Carter inside, still alive and well, though he knew it was a long shot.

"Shh." He put his finger to his lip as they approached the RV and gripped the revolver tight. He crept along its side, his shoulder raised and the barrel aimed at the driver's-side door. He used the side mirror with ever-growing doubt until he approached.

Shit.

Nobody was inside. Not in the front, at least.

"Looks like he ain't home," the boy said, far too loud.

Staring daggers at the kid, Mason swept back to the side door. It was a dangerous risk, but he needed to be sure, so he rapped on the door and listened for any sign of movement inside.

There wasn't a peep.

Mason stepped back and raised the gun.

"No, no, don't—" the boy yelled, holding his ears.

Three bullets blasted the lock at an angle. He shoved open the creaking door, and with his gun raised, he stepped inside.

"You can't do that!" the boy yelled.

Mason continued, fumbling around for a light switch. On the wall to his left, he found something and flicked it. The lights flickered on one at a time, revealing something that Mason could barely believe.

Kylie Carter had told him it was a metal box, and it was exactly that: a cold, empty prison that stank of stale blood. He would have loved to have a black light in here. But it was also quiet, his own echoes the only sounds. "Help me out, kid. Keep shouting until I say stop."

"You can't be in there! There are rules!" he shouted, though it was unclear whether he was meeting Mason's request or displaying real disagreement.

Mason pulled the door to a close, drowning out the sound of the yelling until it was silent. He opened it again and heard him at full volume. *Interesting*, he thought. *It's soundproof. The killer has gone to a lot of trouble to do this.*

"What's going on here?" A large bearded man approached, his chest puffed out.

Mason stepped out from the RV, tucking away the revolver. "I'm a PI, sir. Tracking a killer. Your boy here gave me permission to shoot the lock and go inside."

"That true, boy?" the man snapped.

"What? No! I—" The boy's voice cracked like he was almost crying.

"Go see your momma right now. I'll deal with you later."

The boy disappeared, shooting a middle finger at Mason as he ran.

"Sorry about my son. He can get a little adventurous when I leave him in charge." The man seemed to have a respect for authority, and that would be helpful. "A killer, you say?"

"Yes, sir. He stole this RV and has been keeping it here from time to time. It looks like this is where he brings the abducted children." Mason held out the photograph. "Have you met him before, had any contact at all?"

"Oh, shit." The man—presumably the owner of the yard—looked at the photo. "I knew there was something off about him."

"Off? What makes you say that?"

"Hard to explain. He's just a creepy guy. Look, man..." The guy glanced around as if there were prying ears. "I can let you look in the logbook, but can you keep this from leaking out? This kind of stuff is bad for business."

"Of course. What's in the logbook?"

"My boy didn't show you?" The owner smiled, revealing a small number of black teeth. "When people come through here, we make 'em put down their home address or a contact number. Rules is rules, ya know?"

Mason tried to conceal his excitement. Would the killer have put his real address, or was he smarter than that? Something told Mason he would have to slip up somewhere, and if Mason got lucky, he wasn't far from finding that mistake.

CHAPTER FORTY-TWO

The Lullaby Killer hid behind the scrap heap with clenched fists.

You really are pushing your luck, Mr. Black.

He'd hoped to simply come back and collect his RV but was shocked to see the PI's Mustang parked out front. Perhaps he should have stayed away, but his curiosity made him follow, watching from a distance.

Black had his gun drawn and moved close to the RV, looking to catch him in the act. Soon after, a larger man approached. The killer had spoken with this man before —the owner of the yard. *How can I ever come back here now?*

When the kid stormed off in tears, the killer tried to grab his attention with a low whistle. The boy stopped, looked behind him, then joined the killer at the scrap heap.

"What's going on over there?" he asked the boy.

"That man is looking for you."

"Did he find anything?" The killer peered over the scrap heap and saw Black and the owner heading back toward the reception booth. *This could be a problem.*

"I don't think so."

"All right." He dug into his pockets and took out a ten-dollar bill. You didn't see me here, okay?"

The boy's eyes lit up greedily as he snatched the bill. "Sure."

"Hey, who closes the gates around here?"

"I do, mostly."

The boy seemed eager enough to take money that he might not want to burn his bridges. If he could keep the kid thinking more money would flow his way, he would be under the thumb until the killer said otherwise. He dug around in his pocket for more cash and found another ten dollars. "This is yours if you forget to lock the gate."

With immediate understanding, the boy took the bill. "Yes, sir."

"Good boy. Run along now."

As the kid scurried away with his twenty bucks, the killer had to consider how to get his RV back. He'd gone to far too much trouble to craft the interior that he really didn't want to lose it now—especially at the hands of Mason Black.

Maybe it was time to send the video, to put a wrench in the works. Without a doubt, that would make the investigator stay out of the way for a while. But he was so damn persistent—it seemed as though nothing could make him stop.

You'd better be careful, Mr. Black, the killer thought as he crept around the heap and hopped the fence out of the yard. *Because I know more about you than you do about me.*

CHAPTER FORTY-THREE

I have an address. Mason could barely believe his luck as he climbed back into the Mustang and punched the zip code into the GPS. He was so close he could almost taste it. But he couldn't go alone. He would need backup for this one, and he knew exactly who to call.

He tapped the button on his phone, and Bill answered right away.

"Mason, I'm glad you called," Bill said. "Things are getting tight here."

"Whatever it is, it'll have to wait. I have a potential address for the Lullaby Killer."

"What? That's—Mason, that's fantastic." Bill lowered his head like he was subdued.

Mason turned the key in the ignition. The engine purred. "Right? I didn't want to officially call in the troops, so get down here and help me out, will you?"

"I can't right now. Look, there's been a development."

Mason's heart rate notched up. In the police force,

development was code for *problem*. "Just tell me and get it over with."

"Owen Carter received a ransom video. I'm at his place now, trying to convince him to wait, but he wants to pay it."

"Did you tell him his boy might be dead already?"

"What? No. I can't tell him that."

"You might have to, Bill. If you let it slip that the killer might not play fair, there's a chance he'll hold off on the ransom." It was true, as much of a bastard as it made him feel.

"Tell him yourself, then."

"I'm busy. You know that." Mason put the cell phone on to speaker, dropped it into his lap, and pulled away from the trailer park. Rain was falling again, painting the sky a hazy gray.

"I've been scratching your back. Least you can do is check this out."

Once again, between a rock and a hard place. Mason knew his blurred moral compass needed cleaning. How could he let his ex-partner down, after all this? "Fine," he said, unhappy. "Send forensics to Rigby's trailer park. I'm on my way."

It took almost an hour to reach Owen's place. There were a number of cars on the drive, including Captain Cox's. Mason prepared himself for a *take-your-old-job-back* lecture and went inside without knocking.

"Mr. Black, thank God." Owen stepped forward with a raised cell phone. "You're going to want to watch this." He tapped on the screen and handed it over.

Bill and Captain Cox were gathered around in silence. They'd already seen it, but as always were eager to witness Mason's reaction. Mason, on the other hand, was not looking forward to it at all.

The video showed a young boy with dirty clothes and matted hair. His face was red, as if he'd been crying for days. His cuffed wrists were chained to a pipe as he sat on the floor with his knees to his chest. Other than that, there was nothing to offer.

"Say your name, boy," said a voice from behind the camera.

The boy whimpered and sniffed. *"Ryan Carter."*

"Have I treated you well?"

After a long pause, *"Yes."*

"Show 'em."

Owen walked back into the lounge and slumped into the armchair, sulking and covering his ears. "I can't go through this. Not again."

Mason stood still, the phone held close to his face. This was the first time he'd heard the voice of the Lullaby Killer, and was surprised to hear he had an accent. Kansas, maybe?

"Show 'em!" the man roared, losing his temper.

The Carter boy flinched, then raised a trembling hand. It was easy to make out what was being shown: only three fingers and a thumb. And then the camera panned around in the dark room, making a clunking noise.

"What's with the pinkie fingers?" Bill whispered.

"I don't know," Mason said. "I've never known. Shh."

The camera now pointed at a tray of surgical tools. The statement was clear.

"One million," the killer said. *"Have it ready within three days, and I'll call you. Any later and I'll sing this kid a lullaby. Oh, and Mr. Black..."*

Mason's heart pounded. Had he been watched this whole time?

"Back the fuck off."

The video ended abruptly, turning the screen black. Mason put the phone down and dragged out a kitchen stool. He had a lot to think about. That much was clear.

"What do you think?" the captain asked him. "Shall we arrange the payment? We can do it securely and try to take him down. If we set up away from civilians—"

"Not yet," Mason told her, ignoring the pissed-off look she shot him for being interrupted. "Give me two more days to find this guy, then consider making the payment."

"I don't want any trouble, Mr. Black," Owen said, looking up. "I just want to pay the ransom and have my boy back. One million isn't that much. Not to save my son."

The room fell silent while waiting for Mason to respond. It was good to know he still carried some form of presence and authority, if nothing else. "No," he finally said. "I'll take two days, whether you like it or not. I'm so close. Chances are, the killer just wants the money and will hand over your son. But I wouldn't count on it. This is out of the ordinary for him. Until now, everything he's done was for sport. He doesn't *need* a finger. He just took it because he could."

Mr. Carter wiped his eyes. "Fine. But if my boy dies—"

"Then it'll be on that sick son of a bitch, not on me." Mason's phone rang just before he could lose his temper, but that was forgotten the moment he saw Sandra's name. "What is it?" he asked, holding the phone to his ear.

"Can you come over? It's Amy."

A sweat broke out on Mason's forehead. *Could things get any worse?* "What happened? Is she hurt?"

"Just…" Sandra hadn't sounded this disappointed since she'd announced she wanted a divorce. "It's better you come over here. Please."

Mason sighed. "Won't be long." He hung up and headed for the door. "Two days, Mr. Carter," he called over his shoulder, "and I'll get your boy back."

Bill caught up to Mason just as he reached his car. "Will I see you at home or at the ceremony tomorrow?"

Mason paused. "Ceremony?"

"Missy Daniels's funeral. You *are* going, right?"

Goddamnit. How many more hurdles before he could breach the killer's home? Knowing his luck, it would be a dead end anyway. He opened the door and climbed in. "Is that tomorrow? Jesus. All right, I'll be there," he said, slamming the door and speeding toward his old home.

CHAPTER FORTY-FOUR

Mason was having a tough time juggling the case and his family woes.

As he raced toward the place he used to call home, he pictured all sorts of scenarios for when he'd arrive. As usual, the first was the most dramatic: the killer had been there. But then it evolved into other nightmares, like there had been an accident, or some other medical emergency. As he pulled up at the end of the drive and spotted the patrol cars, he knew he could stop wondering and start worrying.

Climbing the steps with apprehension, Mason reached the front door and let himself in. *Same old Sandra, never locking the front door.* When he entered the hallway, he stopped short, confused by what he saw.

"Don't hate me, Dad."

"Amy?"

His daughter was almost unrecognizable. A number of piercings sparkled on her ghostly-pale face, and her once-beautiful blonde hair had been dyed jet black. Her choice of clothes had changed dramatically, too—tatty laddered stockings and a torn black T-shirt.

"Oh, honey. What've you done?"

Sandra entered the hallway with a police officer at her side. Mason had been the man's superior back on the force, and they'd always seen eye to eye. He tilted his cap. "Mr. Black."

"Rogers, right?"

The officer nodded. "That's right. Sir, I hate to have to tell you that your daughter was caught inside somebody's house. She'd broken in with a friend and was stealing."

Mason could barely believe what he was hearing. "That's not like her."

"It's not that simple!" Amy yelled and banged her way up the stairs and slammed a door. It was as if she'd been taken away and replaced with some angry brat.

There must be more to this. There has to be. "Officer, thank you for your time. I'll have words with her, and it won't happen again. Sandra, see this gentleman out."

The policeman looked as though he wanted to say more, but Sandra's commanding hand on his shoulder led him out. He would've been a fool to say no to her.

"Go on up," Sandra said, her distaste for him no less evident.

Mason headed up the stairs and rapped on the bedroom door. "Amy? I'm coming in, sweetheart." He opened up and saw his daughter lying on the bed, her face buried in a pillow. He closed the door behind him and took a seat next to her. "Tell me."

Amy sobbed and turned her head. Her mascara was running, smudged across her cheeks. "I had a picture of you in my school locker. This girl took it and wouldn't give it back. The teachers didn't care, so I did what I had to do to get it back."

"That's... Honey, there're hundreds of photos of me."

"But this one was *from* you."

Mason knew the photo she was talking about. It was from his younger days, when he and Evie were at college together, arm in arm. It'd been his favorite photo, taken when their parents were still alive.

"Well, here." He leaned to her bedside table and took her phone, flicked on the camera, and raised it up high. "How's this?" He snapped the photo and handed the phone to her.

Amy giggled as she took it. "It's great, Dad."

"Listen, you can't just go breaking into people's houses. You're smarter than that."

"I know. I just got desperate."

"If you get desperate, you come to me. You know I'll do anything for you."

Amy climbed to her knees and threw her arms around her father. "Thanks, Dad."

Mason held her close. After all he'd seen lately, it was nice to be back in this house, even if just for a moment. More than anything, he was just glad Amy was safe. "What's with the clothes anyway?"

"Don't you like it?" She pulled away.

"I do, but it's not *you*, is it?"

Amy looked thoughtful, then shook her head. "I guess not."

After saying goodbye and closing the door, Mason stomped down the stairs to where Sandra stood beside Joshua. "Thank you," she tried to say, but he only nudged his way past.

"Some role model you are."

Mason went to his car and rubbed his eyes. He knew he was in no fit state to approach a serial killer. Besides, if he was reckless and stormed the building and the killer wasn't there, the Carter twin would die for sure. And then there was the matter of Missy Daniels's funeral.

Go to bed, he told himself. *Tomorrow is going to suck.*

CHAPTER FORTY-FIVE

Funerals had never been inviting, but the rain didn't help. Neither did having to watch a mother bury her eight-year-old daughter.

Joanna Daniels was dressed all in black, as was everyone else. She stood over the coffin with a flower in her hand. Mason watched her lower it into the ground and say goodbye.

"Earth to earth," the priest went on. "Ashes to ashes."

Mason could feel himself burning up inside. He thought of the man responsible, the ill-named Lullaby Killer, who'd taken these kids for nothing more than a little fun. It was all a game to him, at least until he'd asked for the money.

As the ceremony drew to a close and the downpour worsened, Joanna Daniels spotted Mason at the back of the crowd. She even looked pretty when she cried, but the beauty and energy she'd once had would never return.

The killer has done this to her, Mason reminded himself.

Joanna approached him, close enough that she was under his umbrella. She was shaking, if not from the cold, then in recognition of her loss. But the way she looked at him—without a hint of warmth—suggested deeper levels of emotion. "Have you caught him?"

"Not yet, ma'am. We're still working on—"

Her shoulder snapped back so fast he didn't see the slap coming. It struck his cheek hard enough to turn his head, and he clutched his face in surprise.

"It's your job, Mr. Black." Joanna began to sob uncontrollably now. "All you had to do was your job, and my little girl would still be alive. This is your fault."

An old man—could have been her father—emerged from behind and eased her away, shooting Mason a look of contempt. It said: *You shouldn't be here.*

Mason had felt the outburst on more than just a physical level.

What if she's right? What if this really is my fault? If I'd just worked harder...

The crowd dispersed, acting as if they hadn't noticed the drama unfolding at the back. People went their separate ways, some to their cars, others walking down the path of the cemetery. They all had their heads down, both out of sadness and respect.

Only one person remained in front of Mason—he hadn't realized she'd come until now, but if anyone could understand how he was feeling, it was Evie.

He just stood there, lost for words.

His sister only looked at him, walked forward, and put a hand on his shoulder. "Don't let that get to you. She's just a woman in tremendous pain. This is not your fault. You hear me?"

Mason stared at her before nodding. He didn't really believe this wasn't a consequence of his own lack of action, but it was a damn sight easier than arguing with the great Evelyn Black. If anything, the slap had served as encouragement to do what needed to be done. "I have somewhere to be. Do you need a ride?"

"Thank you."

Careful not to slide through the mud, Mason and Evie headed toward his car. Although he'd never admit it, he was glad to have her around.

CHAPTER FORTY-SIX

All conversation was saved until the engine stopped. But now it was impossible to keep it locked up inside. Mason craned his neck. "Where have you been?"

Evie lowered her head, wiping her glasses dry with a tissue. "I've been around. Stuff just got in the way, you know? It happens."

Mason wasn't buying it. "I'm not a fool, Evie. At least not when it comes to you. I know it takes something big to keep you away from a case, especially one you fought so hard to get involved in."

Evie slid her glasses back on and watched the droplets of rain rolling down the window. "I had an email from an anonymous sender. Whoever it was, they were threatening Amelia."

"What?" Mason sat up straight.

"Yep. Apparently, if I didn't back off, she would

suffer. So, I went to see her mother... her adoptive mother. She's safe now. That's all that matters."

"Christ, Evie. You should've said something."

"You know I couldn't. You'd have freaked out, like you are now."

They fell silent as Mason accepted she was right. Nobody knew about Amelia. Sure, it was on file somewhere, but spoken words were only between the two of them. "This email. Was it from *him*?"

"It's hard to say. Could be some kid getting his rocks off, but I didn't want to chance it. It was signed off by somebody named Brahm."

As soon as Mason pieced it together, he shook his head, pushing his tongue into the back of his front teeth. "Unbelievable."

Evie shook her head. "What is?"

"Brahms's Lullaby? Man, this guy's ego is off the charts."

"Wow. Okay." Evie drew a deep breath. "Well, how do we know it's not just some kid goofing around, like I said?"

"Right, and how many pimply teenagers know Amelia is your daughter?" For this guy to do all that he'd done, and now to threaten his family? That was unacceptable. Mason would soon put a stop to that. He put the key in the ignition. "So, if you know the girl's safe, do you want back on the case?"

Her hand had already been on the door handle, but now she hesitated. "Fine," she said. "But I'm not writing a damn thing about it. And only if you really, *really* need me."

Mason grinned, started up the engine and punched the killer's address back into the GPS. "Then buckle up."

CHAPTER FORTY-SEVEN

Ryan accepted the Big Mac without hesitation. It was crappy food, but when you haven't eaten in two days you'd take anything. The killer kept the fries as a reward for having collected the RV without being seen. *Wouldn't want to spoil ya.*

Wolfing down the burger in his one good hand, Ryan closed his eyes and twitched with each gulping bite. He was making a hell of a noise, struggling for breath while he took bite after bite like a hungry animal.

The killer knelt down and stared, watching with fascination. "Why don't you like your father?" he finally asked, trying to understand.

Ryan stopped eating and looked at him with wide eyes. "What?"

"You said earlier you didn't like your father. Why is that?"

He looked lost, as though a particular answer was expected. "I just don't."

The killer huffed and sat cross-legged in front of him. This was one way of killing time until the ransom was paid, but boy, did he miss stalking his prey. "Everybody loves their father, unless they're given good reason not to. What's your reason? Tell me, boy."

Scrunching up the hamburger wrapper and dropping it in front of him, the boy burped and covered his mouth with a closed fist. "He likes my sister way more."

This was alarming in every sense of the word. What if he wouldn't pay? What if he'd kept the girl instead? Would he have been able to demand more? *Nah, that's ridiculous. He'll pay.* "What's so special about her?"

"That's what I always ask myself," Ryan said, as if in agreement.

This one seemed incredibly easy to manipulate. *Maybe he can be of use?*

"She's much smarter than I am. Gets all the good grades at school."

"Naw, I wouldn't say that. I think you're plenty smart."

"Really?"

"Sure! Smart, powerful. Here, let me show you something." The Lullaby Killer stood and rummaged through his pocket for the handcuff key. He took two steps back and placed it on the carpet, just out of the kid's reach. "If you can get this key, you won't have to stay cuffed anymore. Deal?"

Ryan Carter hesitated, as if it might be a trick. But like all tempting tricks, he couldn't resist the urge to prove himself. With his free hand, he pulled off his shoe and held the lace in his fist. Leaning as far as he could, he swung the shoe toward the key and tried to hook it.

"See, that's it, smarter than that sister of yours, huh?"

The kid was licking his lips, trying desperately to reach it. When at last it hooked, he dragged the key toward him, picking it up and fumbling it into the cuffs. They fell open with a clink, and Ryan was free.

"Good work!" The killer laughed to encourage him. *So fucking easy!* Even the kid was smiling. "See? Now, why would you let some fool like your daddy tell you there's no brain in that head of yours, huh?"

Although Ryan was grinning now, his head was lowered. "I'm still not tough, either. Not like Kylie. She's tough *and* smart. That's what Dad will say."

The killer kneeled to meet his eye level. "But you're smarter than she is. You just proved it, didn't you? And it's not about being tough. It's about being smart. I bet you... No. That's too risky." He shook his head and turned until he felt the expected hand on his sleeve.

"What?" The boy was far too inquisitive for his own good.

"Well, I bet if you had to hurt someone to save yourself, you could do it."

The boy gave a half nod. "Maybe. But it would have to be to protect myself."

The killer smiled. "See. I knew you were special. Here, come with me." He held out his hand.

"Where are we going?"

"To prove how tough you are, of course."

After staring at him with some skepticism, Ryan took the man's hand, completely unaware he'd been manipulated, and that his innocence was about to be lost.

CHAPTER FORTY-EIGHT

They stood outside the house, ready to kill.

"I'm scared," Ryan said, staring at the door with panic in his eyes.

"Just be smart, boy."

A beautiful woman, no older than thirty, opened the door. The brilliant white smile she flashed them was warm and enchanting, a simple gesture of friendliness.

It soon turned to shock when a gun was aimed at her face.

"Shh." The killer flicked the gun and walked her through the house, leaving the kid to close the door behind them. The woman trembled in fear as she led them into the living room, and she had every reason to be afraid.

They were led into a large room where a squat man with a beer gut sat in awe. The young girl at his feet couldn't have been any older than eight—just a touch younger than Ryan.

"Who are you?" the man asked, raising his hands at the sight of the gun.

"Just a man trying to teach his kid some new skills." The killer pointed the gun at the seat next to him and commanded the woman to sit.

She obeyed, and the girl climbed off the floor and into the man's lap.

"And what's your name, little girl?"

The man protectively wrapped his arms around his daughter. "That's none of your—"

The killer fired the gun at a cushion, and everyone in the room jumped. This was power in his hands, and he would use it to get what he wanted. If anyone chose to get in his way, that was their own problem. "I was asking the girl, not you."

The girl mumbled, "T-Thea."

"Well now," the killer said, moving the gun between both parents, "isn't that a pretty name? Thea, why don't you come and stand over here with me and little Ryan? You'll find it's much, much safer to be on this side of the gun."

"Please don't hurt my family." The woman sobbed, shaking her head.

How pitiful.

"*I'm* not going to do anything. Thea—here, now." He snapped his fingers.

"It's all right, baby," the man said, encouraging her to move.

Thea slid off his lap and stumbled across the living room.

The killer got down on a knee. "Thea, sweetheart. How old are you?"

"E-eight," she stammered, shaking terribly.

"Eight! You're a big girl, then, huh? Tell me, do you love your mom and dad?"

Thea nodded, looking down at her socks.

"Yeah, I bet you do," he said. "Who do you prefer?"

"Please, don't," the woman whimpered, now shuffling into her man's arms.

"It's all right," the killer said, provoking the kid. "Come, whisper it in my ear. I won't tell."

Still not crying, Thea stepped forward and leaned into the killer's ear, whispering as quietly as she could. The killer found this amusing—*everyone* had a favorite parent, just as every parent had a favorite child. They just didn't like to admit it.

"Mommy?" The killer yelled her secret. "You prefer Mommy?" And with a slight jerk of the hand, he aimed the gun at the woman and squeezed the trigger. The bullet exploded from the barrel and her face froze in shock, then she looked down at the patch of red spreading at her gut.

"You son of a bitch!" The man leapt to his feet, tears welling in his eyes. He'd reacted even more strongly than his daughter, who only sobbed quietly to herself.

"Sit the fuck down," the killer said. "Right now, or I'll make this *very* painful for you."

The man hesitated, then sat beside his dead wife.

"Ryan, you're up."

The boy shuffled forward, also shaking, and undoubtedly vulnerable now.

Chuckling, the killer placed the gun in his hand. "You want to feel that power? It's easy. You have the power in your hand, therefore you *are* the power. You see what we did here tonight? I bet this man would do anything to make sure his daughter is safe."

Ryan chewed his lip.

"Go ahead, ask him."

He stared at the floor, trying to think of something to say, then looked up, pointing the gun at the crying man whose life had been destroyed only moments ago. "Poke yourself in the eye," Ryan said but made it sound like a question.

"W-What?"

"You heard the kid," the killer said. "Do as you're told."

Creasing his brow, the man lifted a quivering finger in front of his face, then jammed it into his tear-soaked eye. He screamed a curse as he did so, then covered his eye with his hand.

Ryan began to laugh hysterically. "That's funny!"

"That's right," the killer told him. "And you made him do it by coming here with me and holding the gun. What does that mean?"

"Hmm. That I'm... smart?"

"Exactly!" The killer applauded him, taking his hands off Thea for only an instant. "Now, shoot the man, or I'll shoot you."

"What?"

"You heard me. You said you could kill to protect yourself. I'm telling you now that you'll die if you don't kill this man." *And I might just be walking out of here alone.*

Ryan made a sound that kids do when they're terrified. "I... I don't think I can."

"Oh, sure you can. Just point and shoot. Pretend he's your daddy. Remember him? The one who kept making you feel stupid? The one who kept saying you're nothing compared to your sister?" He kneeled, leaning close to the boy's ear. "The daddy who isn't even looking for you? Pretend this is him, and let him know how you feel."

"You're a fucking bastard!" Ryan screamed at the man through gritted teeth, imagining his father as instructed. "I hate you!"

"Again," the killer demanded. "Tell him again."

"I *hate* you! *I hate you!*"

"Shoot him!"

The gun went off in Ryan's hand, then dropped to the floor with a clunk. The girl screamed at the deafening gunshot and tried to run, but the killer held her shoulder tighter.

"Yes!" He hadn't expected the boy to cave in so soon, but it was beautiful.

"What did I do?" Ryan asked, stumbling back toward the wall.

"You showed your true strength, kid. But the real question is, what to do with little Thea? What do you think, hmm?"

The girl wriggled and struggled, trying to escape the killer's grasp.

With tears in his eyes, Ryan looked at her thoughtfully.

Then he made his decision.

CHAPTER FORTY-NINE

Mason headed up the path with Evie at his side and the revolver in his pocket.

"You sure this is the right place? It looks too neat."

Mason's gaze swept across the ceramic gnomes dotted across the lawn and the water feature that stood in the center of the grass. *She might be right,* he thought, *but that doesn't mean we shouldn't be careful.*

They knocked on the door, Mason keeping his finger coiled around the trigger.

"Just let me do the talking," Evie told him.

An elderly woman opened the door, surprising them both. She was tall, with gray hair and purple-rimmed glasses. Were it not for her confusion at the serious-looking couple on her doorstep, she might have been more welcoming. "Yes?"

Evie paused. "I'm sorry, we were expecting a man."

"Last I checked, dear, I was all woman."

Mason took over, handing over a picture of the killer.

"Do you recognize this man? His RV has been linked to this address."

The woman shook her head. "Oh, dear. What has he been up to now?"

"So you *do* know him," Evie said.

"Perhaps you should come in." The woman opened up the door and allowed them entry, then showed them into the living room where far too many cats ran around freely.

Mason clutched the gun, still unsure about trusting the old lady.

"I'm afraid the man you're looking for is my son," she said, as if revealing a dirty secret.

Her son? It wasn't exactly what they'd been looking for, but it sure was better than nothing. He looked at Evie, who seemed as surprised as he was, then back at the woman. "Could we please take his full name, age, and anything else you can dig up?"

"If you tell me what this is about, dear, you can have anything you like."

"We're investigating a series of murders and have reason to believe your son is involved somehow. We'd just like to ask him a few questions," Mason lied.

The woman's jaw dropped in horror. "*My* son?"

"I'm afraid so."

"I always worried something like this might happen. Hold on a moment." She disappeared from the room, leaving Mason and Evie to catch their breath. She soon returned with papers, handing them straight over. "Just a few things I could find."

Mason flicked through them, handing some to Evie. There was so much of use here. Wage slips from hardware stores dating back to a couple years ago, Social Security numbers, phone bills and the like. Even a name: Marvin Wendell. It was very valuable information, but it still wasn't a set of handcuffs over the killer's wrists.

"I just wish I could be more help," Mrs. Wendell said.

"When was the last time you saw your son?" Mason asked, looking up at her.

"Oh, not for some years now. He never really liked me much."

"Why's that, Mrs. Wendell?"

She gazed out the window, as if struggling to recall. "He was a very angry boy. You see, I once had a man in my life who was very firm with him. I remember he once chased my son through the house. My little Marvin tried to hide behind a door when my boyfriend swung it open. Took his whole finger off." She wiggled her pinkie finger. "I think he always blamed me for that."

"This is our guy," Mason said, fighting to contain his excitement. Evie nodded along with him. *It's really him. And that would explain the mutilation*, he thought. It was probably the reason he always wore gloves, too. "Mrs. Wendell, could I perhaps have a glass of water?"

The woman nodded but looked as if she'd grown tired of the conversation already. As soon as she left the room, Mason stood and opened a nearby drawer, rummaging through it. There was nothing of use.

"I can't believe we've identified him," Evie said,

looking around the room behind him. "It seems too good to be true, after all these years."

"I'm glad you think so, too." Mason kept looking around until he saw the photo frame on a high shelf. He took it down and studied it. The picture showed a bearded man in his early twenties with a missing finger. He stood next to a slightly younger version of his mother. "Looks like the same guy."

Evie came up behind him and took the photo.

"Looks like we have everything except a location," he said without looking back. "What do you think?" When Mason turned, he saw the horrified look he'd only seen from his sister a handful of times. "What's wrong?"

"I didn't spot it before, but this photo is clearer." She looked up from the photograph. "Mason... I know this man."

CHAPTER FIFTY

"Okay, pull in here," Evie said, guiding him from the passenger seat.

"Care to explain why you've brought me to this shithole?" Mason stopped the car and climbed out, following his sister toward an old, rundown building.

"A few years ago I was moonlighting for a magazine that barely made it off the ground. I used to collect information, but now and then I had to sit in on some interviews."

Mason held the office door for her. "That's how you know this Marvin guy?"

"Exactly. I didn't recognize the newer pictures, as he hasn't aged well. And that beard..."

Inside the narrow corridor, they walked to the front desk where a stocky man with no hair rose to his feet. "I'll be goddamned. That ain't Evelyn Black? It couldn't be."

"Hi, Geoff." Evie hugged the man, then stepped back and introduced her brother.

"A private investigator?" he asked, sounding impressed, although it was probably just a case of good manners. "And what brings you back to the seventh circle of hell?"

"I need a favor, actually," Evie explained, showing him the photo they'd stolen from Mrs. Wendell when she wasn't looking. "Do you remember when we interviewed this guy? I think he wanted the key researcher job, if I remember correctly."

"Remember him? Sweet thing, I still see him."

"You do?" Evie's voice pitched up a notch.

Mason hung back. It seemed as though she had this one covered. He was beginning to think deciding to help each other out had been a good move after all.

"That's right. We didn't give him the job, but he keeps coming back and asking if we have some information on a string of murders or something." Geoff rubbed at his beard.

"The Lullaby Killer?"

"That's the one!" Geoff said. "I had no idea what he was talking about until I googled it. Seemed like something I was better off not knowing about."

"A reporter with a conscience," Evie jested.

"Still a comedienne, I see."

Evie smiled. "Do you know where we might find him?"

"I'm afraid not. Well, actually..." The man glanced awkwardly at Mason. "I, uh... A friend of mine says he saw him over at Keira's once or twice. It might be worth poking around there, so to speak."

"Who's Keira?"

"*Keira's*," Mason corrected, pushing himself away from the wall with his elbows. "It's a strip club. Geoff, thank you for your time. And offer our gratitude to your friend." He gave a playful wink and headed for the door.

Evie said goodbye and caught up to Mason, almost being pushed aside by a goofy teenager bursting in from outside.

"It's that killer I was talking about, Geoff!" the teen yelled across the hall.

Mason and Evie stopped, listening in.

"I told you to let that go," Geoff said, his voice booming.

"But he's struck again! Some public display over on Cadwallader Street."

Mason looked at Evie and saw his own panic reflected in her eyes. They sprinted to the Mustang and climbed in, determined not to miss a beat.

CHAPTER FIFTY-ONE

"I'll be here if you need me."

Mason left Evie in the car and pushed his way through the mass of curious bystanders. They all seemed to be testing how long they could look at it before their gag reflexes kicked in, but Mason was yet to understand what it was they were looking at.

When he finally got to the front of the crowd, his heart sank to his stomach.

The front window had the drapes drawn two-thirds of the way, and in the middle hung a young girl's body silhouetted against the light behind. Her legs dangled motionlessly, and her eyes were open and full of pain.

"Jesus." Mason ducked under the police tape and showed his badge to a nearby officer.

"I'm afraid I can't let you in," he said, using his palm as a barricade.

What the hell? "Step aside, Officer, or I'll break every bone in that hand."

The officer's eyes narrowed. "What did you just say to me?"

"I said step aside or—"

"Mason!" Bill stepped out of the house and came over. "You just saved me a phone call. Come on in." He appeared not to have noticed the hostile exchange.

"Next time," Mason whispered to the officer as he passed and headed inside, where Captain Cox was barking orders at a swarm of forensic investigators. When she laid eyes on Mason, she offered the weakest of courtesy smiles.

"Over here." Bill led him to the nearest wall, where something had been scrawled in blood.

"Surprised you didn't draw the drapes. You're putting on quite a display there."

"Cap doesn't want anything touched on the scene until forensics are done. It's not what I'd have done, but we have to follow the rules."

Mason, trying not to let his curious eye sway toward the girl, followed Bill and looked directly at the wall. He mouthed the words as he read what was inscribed in blood: *OFTEN THROUGH MY CURTAINS PEEP*.

"Twinkle, Twinkle?" Bill asked, beating him to the punch.

"Right." Mason knew he shouldn't do it, but it was a necessity, and he looked at the girl's hand for confirmation that this was the Lullaby Killer. When he saw a single drop of blood leak from where the girl's finger had once been, he thought of something.

"Can I get a black light?"

"You think—"

"Please, Bill, it's been a long day. Just get me a black light."

Bill whistled to a nearby techie and made the request. It wasn't long before Mason was turning it on and holding it up against the text.

"We know it's her blood," Bill said. "We swabbed it already."

Mason shined the UV against the wall and looked all around the area. "But you didn't see this, did you?" He pointed at a small handprint on the wall. It was the size of a young child's.

"We missed that," Bill confessed with shame.

"I don't think it's the girl's."

"What? Why?"

Mason demonstrated against the air. "I think someone else did this, leaning against the wall while they wrote with the severed finger. Check the prints, see if they match." Mason handed the black light over and took a few steps back. *This guy is sick.*

Mason had barely accepted what he'd seen before Captain Cox appeared at his side. "What do you make of the parents?" she asked. She'd always respected his opinion and had no trouble telling him as much, but he thought she might have a clue of her own by now. After all, she was the youngest person in San Francisco to have ever made captain.

"I haven't spoken to them yet."

Cox screwed up her face. "Wait, you don't know?"

Mason shook his head, sensing this was about to get a whole lot worse.

The captain walked him to two nearby gurneys, unzipped the body bags and showed the faces of a young couple, one of which had a gunshot wound in the center of his forehead, the woman with one in her stomach.

"These were found here?" Mason leaned in close, desperate to find some sort of explanation.

"Right over there on the couch. Still think this is the Lullaby Killer?"

"Without a doubt. I just... This isn't like him. It's as if he was rushed, or—"

"Or what?"

Mason was drowning out the sounds of everyone around him. It was the way he'd trained himself to make a scenario from a jumble of clues in order to reach a conclusion. Suddenly it twigged. "The boy."

"What?" asked Bill and Captain Cox in unison.

"It was the boy." Mason looked up, feeling more sickened than he ever had before. "I think he made Ryan Carter do this."

CHAPTER FIFTY-TWO

Ryan was shown into the dark room. The door slammed shut behind him.

"Wasn't that great, boy?" the killer asked him, but it sounded rhetorical.

Ryan felt an unfamiliar feeling inside, a distasteful cocktail of sadness and shame. How had be been persuaded to do such a horrible thing? In that moment it had seemed like a good idea, but now? His father would never be able to look at him if he found out what he'd done.

"Hey, I'm talking to you."

Ryan shrugged, taking a seat on the floor where he knew he belonged.

The killer looked down at him like he'd been insulted. "You don't feel smart? You don't feel powerful? What the hell's a matter with ya?"

"I feel... bad."

"Well, tough shit. You did something today that your

dad could never be proud of because he only gives a damn about your sister. But listen here," the killer said as he crouched in front of him, "*I'm* proud of you."

Ryan smiled at him, but only because he knew it was the easiest way of shutting him up. By now he was learning the best ways to avoid further aggression. "Thank you."

The killer rose. "Good boy. Now stay here and watch TV. I need to run out and do something. But don't you get up off that floor, ya hear?" He switched on the ancient TV and headed out, closing the door.

He didn't lock it. Ryan sat staring at the door, ignoring the cartoons on the television. *I could try now, unless... Is it a test?* That hopeful part of him said to get up and try, but the angel on his shoulder told him he'd better stay put.

But it can't hurt to check, can it?

His hand hurt as he pushed himself off the floor and crept across the room. *Perhaps just a little peek won't matter*, he convinced himself. If the killer was still there, he could just say that he was making sure he was safe inside.

Yeah, that's not a bad idea.

Embracing the fear, he wrapped his good hand around the knob. Trying his damndest not to shake, he twisted it and gave it a pull. To his surprise, it clicked open, and a cold autumn breeze assaulted his face.

Ryan poked his head through the door and winced.

Up the walkway, the killer stood enjoying a cigarette, blowing a cloud of smoke into the air. He had his back to the room but could turn at any moment. And then the punishments would begin.

Pushing the door to a close, Ryan pondered how fast he could run. If only he could make it to the street, he could cry for help and get out of there before the killer even noticed.

But it was risky.

Well, Ryan asked himself, *what's it going to be?*

CHAPTER FIFTY-THREE

It was the hardest decision of his life, but it was his only hope.

Ryan darted out of the room as fast as his legs could carry him. He was barely off the property when he heard the killer shouting after him.

"Boy? Boy! Jesus Christ."

He didn't want to look back, to see the man catching him up. All he could do was ignore the shooting pains in his legs and push forward.

Ryan hit the street, bare on each side here but with a variety of bars and houses farther up the road. He tried his hardest to sprint faster, to reach the public places sooner. And then he heard the RV behind him.

The killer sounded the horn, startling Ryan. It was close behind him, but how close? Close enough to hear the engine roaring, that was for sure. The cold breeze brought tears to Ryan's eyes as he ran, making snot dribble from his nostrils, but he was almost at the lively street.

"Help!" he screamed, realizing with horror there was not another human being in sight.

The RV closed in behind him, tormenting him rather than stopping him.

Should I stop? The devils of simple submission were playing a number on him, telling him the easy option was just to return and accept his punishment. *No, I need to get home, even if my dad still hates me.*

Ryan's toe hit the curb, sending him tumbling to the ground. He brought his hands up just in time to guard his face, but his knees and elbows took an agonizing, damaging blow. He winced, hearing the RV revving even closer and the killer shouting out the window.

"Don't make me get out of this vehicle!"

Panicking, Ryan picked himself up and disappeared into a nearby alleyway, not stopping to dust himself off. As he rounded the corner, he saw something only God could have sent, to save him from his captor.

"Help!" he screamed to the two men at the end of the alley. "Please help!"

The men stepped forward. One was black and wearing sports gear, in spite of the cold, while the other man, slightly older, wore a business suit. They looked an odd pair to be hanging out in an alley, but Ryan wasn't about to complain.

"What's going on here?" the younger one asked. It looked like he was zipping up his fly.

"Someone's chasing me," Ryan wheezed.

The killer entered the alleyway and caught up to them, smiling and wiping his forehead. "Sorry, fellas, my boy's just being a bit dramatic. You know how it is."

"This your son?" the old man asked, crooking an eyebrow and pushing his chest out.

"Oh sure, yeah." The killer looked down at Ryan. "Come on. Let's go home."

But the men weren't buying it—something about the crying child suggested he wasn't simply disobeying his father. The old man stood in the way. "Sorry, sir, but you're going to have to prove—"

With lightning speed, the killer drew a gun from the back of his pants and fired a quick shot into each of the men. They landed to either side of Ryan, making him squeal with horror.

"Nice try, kid," the killer said, spitting as he stowed the gun away. "Just when I thought I could trust you."

Ryan jerked back as the man grabbed him, dragging him back to the RV.

CHAPTER FIFTY-FOUR

Mason got back in his car and told Evie what he'd seen. He was watching her expression as she digested the information, mostly to see if it affected her as much as it had him.

"It's hard to see the bright side, but this suggests Ryan Carter is still alive, right?"

"Yeah, but try telling his father that. Look, I need to pay Mr. Carter a visit. Do you think you can head to Keira's, see what you can dig up?"

"It's a strip club, for Christ's sake. Couldn't you—"

"Can you go or not?" Mason snapped.

"Fine. Whatever. As long as I can take the car."

Mason reached into his pants pocket and grabbed a handful of cash, then held it out to her. "For the cab fare."

Evie stared at it, then snatched it and left. "Be careful."

Mason made his way to the Carter household, wondering how the man would take the news. Moreover, how would Mason phrase it? *Sorry, sir, but your son mutilated a young girl? Your boy is alive, but he's working with the killer?* Something was amiss, but what it was eluded him completely.

Owen opened the door and showed him in, but Mason only stood in the hallway.

"What is it?" Owen asked, clearly expecting bad news.

He has no idea. "It's not much of an update," Mason said, speaking slow and trying not to further upset the man, "but I think your son is still alive. For now."

Owen sniffed and wiped his eyes, then looked up. "That's great though, right? That means I can pay the ransom and get my son back."

Mason shook his head. "I still don't think it's that simple."

"I don't understand. Why can't I just pay the money and have my son? I don't care about the million dollars. I just want to see Ryan and tell him that I'm sorry."

"Because you have to think about the other children, Mr. Carter. If you pay that money, a serial killer goes free. Whose kids will be next? I don't give a damn about your million, either. I just want the killer in cuffs, if not —" Mason caught sight of young Kylie cowering by the upstairs banister. It was good to see her out of the hospital, and he couldn't blame her for wanting to know where her twin brother was. "If not dead."

"But my son dies regardless?"

"Not at all. You know we're trying to—"

"Trying to what? To catch a killer at any cost, including my boy's safety?"

"Hey, now you listen here," Mason snapped, trying to ignore his guilt at speaking harshly to a man with a missing child. He knew that if Amy had been abducted instead, he would slit throats to get her back. "You're trying to counter everything I say with the same comment. You're going to give me one more day. I'm close, Mr. Carter. I just know it."

"How close?" Owen asked, pleading with his eyes.

"Close enough." Mason headed for the door.

"What if I—"

"One more day!" Mason closed the door and sucked in the fresh air, steadying his nerves. Time was not on his side, and he knew it.

CHAPTER FIFTY-FIVE

Evie maneuvered between the tables of perverted creeps.

It wasn't her kind of scene—everything from the sleazy music to the down-and-out women flashing their skin, bringing shame on ladies everywhere who were trying to make a decent living. *But still*, she thought, *people do what they have to.*

Arriving at the empty bar, she flashed a photo of Marvin Wendell to the bartender. "Do you know this guy?" she asked.

He polished an assortment of shot glasses one by one, staring at the photo until recognition settled in. "Might have seen him. Who's asking?"

"Evelyn Black. I'm a private investigator, of sorts."

Flicking the cleaning cloth over his shoulder, the barman assessed her for a moment before dialing a number on a landline. He kept one eye on her, explaining to the person on the phone what was happening.

Now why would you need to make a call?

Evie glanced around her, studying the men in black suits who stood bolt upright and scanned their surroundings. When she'd first come in, she'd thought they were bouncers, but now she finally understood: they were bodyguards.

Two of them approached her, one of whom had a finger to his earpiece.

"Miss Black? Come with us."

Evie swallowed hard and followed them through to the back, wishing she'd taken the gun from Mason's car. They were backstage, heading up a set of creaking wooden stairs until they reached a door, where the bigger bodyguard punched in a code and showed her inside.

"Miss Black, is it?" A ponytailed man in his forties sat at his desk, shuffling some things into a drawer.

Evie tapped her nose and flicked her head at him, letting him know some powder remained beside his nostril. Embarrassed, the man understood and brushed the cocaine from his nose. He sniffed, to make sure.

"I hear you're asking about a guy."

Glancing around and trying not to freak out that they'd closed the door behind her, Evie approached the desk and showed the picture of Wendell. "Some say he comes here often?"

The man studied the photo, then glanced up at Evie before speaking with that croaky Manhattan accent. "What are you, police?"

"A PI, actually."

"Right, right. Can I see your credentials?"

Shit. Evie knew she should have borrowed Mason's badge. She'd done that on multiple occasions in the past—it was surprising just how many people saw the shiny brass and looked no further. "I left them at home."

The man laughed, and his bodyguards followed suit. "You can see the trouble here, miss. A young woman such as yourself comes in here asking questions about a paying customer, has no identification, and yet wants information. How do you think that looks?"

Evie, trying to conceal her shaking hands, cleared her throat. "Look, I'm trying to pretend this is *just* a strip joint, and that I couldn't head downstairs right now and hire one of your whores." She licked her dry lips, shuffled her weight to the other foot. "I'm not a dyke, but I'd do it just to prove a point. Listen. *This* man is dangerous." She pointed at the photo. "He's killed before, and he'll do it again. So unless you want the police at your door, how about you show me some professional courtesy?"

The smile fell from the man's face in an instant, but he didn't speak as he paused for thought.

"Well?" Evie prompted, fake courage to the fore.

"Miss Black, this is the only courtesy you'll get from me: turn around and go back to whichever hole you crawled out from. Never come back here. If you do, even the police won't be able to protect you. You hear?"

It sounded to Evie like a generous offer. It was obvious he wasn't going to give up any details, so what other choice did she have than to walk out while she still could?

Without another word, she took the door and headed

back downstairs, where the music had picked up its tempo and some skinny redhead was sliding out of her panties on stage. Men were hollering and whistling like a pack of excited dogs.

Evie kept her head down and went for the exit, keeping a cautious eye over her shoulder. She almost screamed when she walked into the stripper.

"Easy there," said a topless blonde, feeding a scrap of paper into her hand while glancing over her shoulder. She walked away without looking back.

Evie knew better than to open it in plain sight, and made for the exit and darted around to the side. Nervous and curious, she unfolded the note and read the message with its one clear instruction: *Meet me out back at midnight.*

CHAPTER FIFTY-SIX

Midnight was approaching, but not fast enough. Evie hugged herself in the cold alleyway, refusing to take her eyes off the filthy old man taking a piss behind the dumpster.

He zipped up and stumbled drunkenly toward her.

"Want some fuh-fun, gorgeous?" he asked as he swayed from side to side.

"I'm not here for that." Evie took a step back, disgusted.

"You don't want—" He burped. "—some of this?"

The club's back door swung open and the stripper who'd left the message stepped out. It was a complete transformation to see her in clothes. Inside she'd looked like a whore who'd do anything for money. Now she looked like somebody's mom. "Go home, Jeremy," she said to the drunk.

He turned, oblivious to what was going on, then

stumbled into the darkness while muttering incoherent words.

"Sorry about him," the stripper said, stepping closer.

"Thanks for the rescue." Evie held up the note. "You have some information?"

The stripper chewed on her gum. "You a cop?"

Evie believed this woman deserved the truth, at least. "Just an interested party."

After a longer stare of assessment, the stripper took Evie by the arm and led her away from the club, lowering her voice. "That man you've been looking for? His name's Marvin Wendell. He comes here a lot."

She knows his name. At least I know she's not lying to me. "You've danced for him?"

The stripper laughed. "My profession extends a little further than just dancing, if you catch my drift. Wendell is a client of mine. Into some freaky shit, but he always pays."

"Have you been in his RV?"

"RV? Sweetheart, we catch a cab to a motel up the road. Romero's, I think it's called."

Evie wasn't at all surprised the man was into prostitution. "Are you sure it's him?"

"Couldn't be surer. Guy was missing a finger. Kind of reduces the pleasure, if you get what I'm saying." The stripper winked. She was a friendly woman, kind of overkeen to please but generally big-hearted.

"I get you," Evie said, avoiding her gaze. "You say he pays you. Is he wealthy?"

They passed the drunk they'd seen only moments

ago, now sleeping it off on a nearby bench that was still wet from the recent showers. The street was otherwise empty.

"He pays me for the whole night because of the distance to the motel. It suits me—I don't have much of a life outside this place anyway, and I'm saving to go back to college."

Evie felt for the woman, but what could she do? "Romero's. Got ya. Thanks for your help...?"

"Jennifer."

"Jennifer. You take care." Evie handed her the cab money Mason had provided, smiled, and walked toward the nearest bus stop to wait for her brother. She had a feeling he'd be more than a little interested in the new information.

CHAPTER FIFTY-SEVEN

Mason pulled up to the bus stop to find his sister shivering with cold and clearly tired. It was getting late, and she'd probably want to head home.

"Evie," he called over and let her in the car. They parked to talk about the latest, and even took a cigarette from the emergency supply and shared it while catching up on the details.

"So, this Wendell guy," Mason said, taking a long, smoky draw. "He uses this motel often?"

"All the time, apparently."

"Why not use the RV?" Since Mason had discovered it at Rigby's and the LAPD had shown up to retrieve it, it'd been collected by its owner. He could've kicked himself for not having it impounded sooner.

"You said it yourself," Evie said, taking the cigarette from him and tapping the spent ash into the Mustang's tray, "it has no real interior. Just a tin can, right?"

It was true. But however much Mason wanted to

believe Marvin Wendell would be at the motel, he had his doubts. "You coming, or do you want me to drop you home?"

Evie cracked a window and tossed the butt outside. "You're going now?"

"I don't want to waste any more time."

"But you're exhausted, and it's a couple of hours outside the city."

"I'll live." Mason knew exactly where this was headed: the ever-persistent request that she get to drive his precious Mustang. He didn't like it—never had—but it made sense on this occasion. "Just be gentle with her, all right?"

Evie climbed out and they swapped seats. Mason reclined in the passenger seat as Evie struggled to handle the unfamiliar power of the car. He wanted to get some shut-eye—he really did—but it was impossible to relax with Evie grinding the gears.

After an hour had passed, the car was being handled better, so Mason lay back, his eyes on the sky. Was he on his way to meet Wendell, or would it be another dead end? And what about Ryan Carter? He didn't want to admit it, but the odds weren't in the boy's favor.

This could be the last night the boy ever lives, he thought as he watched the passing yellow blur of streetlights. He only hoped he was wrong.

CHAPTER FIFTY-EIGHT

The motel was a rundown mess of a place, fit for a horror movie.

Mason was first out the car, leaving Evie trailing behind as he rushed inside to talk with the clerk. The moment he entered, he was faced with a sweaty middle-aged man who looked as sleazy as he did greasy.

"Looing for a room?" the clerk asked without looking up.

"No, actually, I'm looking for a guest." He placed his badge on the counter and pushed it onto the man's smut magazine, forcing him to look at it. "Goes by the name Wendell."

"Customer confidentiality. They have their right to privacy, and I'm loyal to that." The clerk shoved the badge back over and returned to his "reading," rude and uninterested.

"The man's a killer." Mason flipped up the counter and invited himself in. He was aware of Evie entering the building when the bell jingled. But even she knew better than to get involved in this conflict.

"Hey, you can't come back here!" The man stood up, but Mason's hand guided him back down by his throat. He slumped into his chair, his cheeks growing rosy red.

Mason perused the bookshelf until he found a row of binders and ledgers, each labeled in date order. He took the most recent out, slid it into his large palm, and scanned through for the name. Wendell wasn't listed, but another name caught his attention: *Brahm*.

Mason wondered whether the killer was using the name as a cover, or if he was cruelly mocking them, leaving a trail of breadcrumbs all the way to a dead end.

"Put that down!" the clerk yelled without standing up.

"Not until I meet this guy." Mason looked at the attached sign-in sheet, following the point of his finger across the columns of the spreadsheet. "He's here now?"

"Depends," the clerk said, rubbing his throat. "What's it to you?"

"Everything."

"Look, man, the guy comes, pays ahead, and asks for privacy. We don't speak."

Mason shrugged him off and looked at the room number. "Evie, room seven."

"Now, wait a minute." The clerk rose, standing only for Mason to shove him back down again. "You can't just waltz in here like you own the place. I'll need to see—"

But Mason didn't want to hear it. He slid the key for room seven off the hook and marched outside, Evie a few steps ahead of him. The clerk was hobbling behind, protesting his guest's right to privacy.

"Over here," Evie said, stopping outside the room.

"If you go in there, I'm calling the police," the clerk said, folding his arms.

"Go ahead," Mason told him. "Ask for Detective Bill Harvey." He slid the key into the door and jerked it. It put up a little resistance but finally clicked and creaked open. He was expecting to be faced with the infamous Lullaby Killer but instead found something far worse.

Evie stood beside him and squinted into the dark room, their jaws both dropping at once.

What they saw was enough to give them nightmares for the rest of their lives.

CHAPTER FIFTY-NINE

"Hurry up with that police call," Mason yelled at the clerk. "Request an ambulance, too!"

The smell was unreal: sweat, blood and something musty. As dark as it was inside, it was clear enough to see the boy, beaten black and blue and sprawled out across the bed. He looked dead, and even if he wasn't, he wouldn't live much longer.

"Wait here," he told Evie, stepping inside and grabbing the lamp off the cabinet. He wrapped the cord around his fist and gripped the lamp, moving to the adjoining room with his back to the wall. Anyone could be in here, he knew, and he would have to clear it before he could tend to the boy.

Steeling himself, Mason pushed open the door to what was a clean bathroom. The lights were on, but nobody was inside. He tried not to touch too much—this was a crime scene, and he didn't want to contaminate it any more than he'd have to.

The next door was only a closet, with nothing inside but spare linen. Assured now they were alone, Mason dropped the lamp and ran to the boy, looking down at his body. There was blood on his shirt, right around the belly.

Mason checked for a pulse but felt nothing.

"Ugh!" The boy gasped, one last desperate ounce of life returning to him.

Mason ripped the pillowcase off a nearby pillow, scrunched it up, and pressed it to the boy's wound. It looked like a knife tear. "Ryan Carter? You need to hang in there, okay? We're going to get you to a hospital." It may have been falling on deaf ears, but he imagined this was his own daughter, and nothing would stop him from trying.

"Stand back," he called to Evie, lifting the kid in his arms and taking him outside. He needed air, space, and to get away from the crime scene. Lowering Ryan onto the ground, he held up his head.

"My God. What happened?" Evie asked, stunned.

"He's been stabbed. He's dehydrated, too. Where's that ambulance?"

Evie disappeared to a nearby wall and opened up the ice dispenser.

The clerk returned with a phone in his hand. "I called them. It's on its way. Hey, is that little boy gonna be okay?"

"He'd fucking well better be!" Mason was losing it. He couldn't let the Lullaby Killer win. Not at the cost of this young boy, nor any other.

Evie returned with a bottle of water, trickling it between the boy's lips.

"Easy. Don't choke him," Mason said.

"I wasn't going to. Hey, look." Evie pointed at the boy's hand, where a reddened bandage barely covered the absence of his pinkie finger.

That son of a bitch, Mason thought.

Little Ryan Carter groaned, rolled his head to one side, and stopped breathing.

"No," Mason said, his energy failing him. "Please, no." And as he held the dying boy in his arms, all he could imagine was the face of Owen Carter as he told him he'd failed to save his son.

CHAPTER SIXTY

The Lullaby Killer had been scoping out a new victim. He'd named this activity the School Run, and there'd been plenty to choose from. With that in mind, he'd even considered moving to the other side of San Francisco to carry out his work.

Stay unpredictable.

With the Carter twin put down once and for all, he now had the time to think about a new lullaby. *It was a nice touch*, he thought as he pulled onto the empty stretch of road. These little enigmas kept the police guessing—kept *Mason Black* guessing—for a number of years. And while they'd wasted their time trying to find some sort of a hint within the madness of his signatures, he'd simply run off into the sunset.

Wendell even liked the name; *the Lullaby Killer* had a nice ring to it.

The RV was a bitch to drive, but it got the job done.

He continued up the road to collect the twin's body so he could keep it concealed until the ransom was paid.

The thought of the money excited him. He could go anywhere. Do anything. All of the greatest killers in America's history had moved around the map—some of whom had never been caught. He could become one of them. *One of the greats.*

"Oh, no," he said aloud as he saw what was in the distance. "Oh. Fucking. No."

Ahead of him, a host of police cars surrounded Romero's Motel.

Wendell tried to tell himself they hadn't found the body, but of course they had. Why else would they be there? He slowed down just enough to see the commotion without drawing attention upon himself.

You again. His blood began to boil at the very sight of him. *Mason Black.* Every time there was a bump in the road, this guy was right there. *Why can't you just leave it alone, huh?*

Registering the ambulance as he drove past, and seeing the Carter kid being lifted into it, he pictured his million dollars disappearing down a deep well. With his escape gone and a new plan in mind, he carried straight on down the road.

You're on thin ice, Mr. Black.

CHAPTER SIXTY-ONE

The ambulance arrived in record time, but Bill and Owen had taken longer.

"We think he's going to be fine," the paramedic said. "We'll just get him to the hospital and have him all patched up."

Bill thanked the EMTs and sent them on their way, while forensics and police officers fluttered around them to examine the crime scene. "You did good, Mason."

"I don't think so," he said. "The killer's still out there. We may have spilled the glass, but the bottle is still poisoned." He turned back to the room where Ryan Carter had been bleeding out only a few minutes ago. He thought about how close he'd been to losing another child and shivered.

"Mr. Black," Owen called, stepping away from the ambulance and hopping over the puddles. "I have to follow them back to the hospital, but I wanted to come and thank you." He held out a hand and shook with Mason. "Please contact me about your fee. That million I was going to pay up, it's yours if you want it."

Evie had stood quietly until now. "Take it."

Mason shook his head. "You're just light-headed from seeing your boy again. Keep the money and scratch the bill. This has never been about the payday."

Owen's expression turned serious, as did Bill's and Evie's. "Both of my kids were abducted, and they were both returned to me alive. I'm the luckiest man on the planet." All smiles, he headed back to his car and followed the ambulance.

"That's some seriously good work, Mason," Bill said.

"It was mostly Evie, you know." Mason patted her on the back, pushing her into the spotlight, and stomped back toward his Mustang.

"Where're you going?" Bill called after him.

"The hospital. That boy needs to give a statement when he comes around." It wasn't something he was proud of, but Mason understood they'd just deprived a serial killer of a million bucks and knew that if that were him, he'd be looking for vengeance.

"Christ, buddy. Take a day off. Recharge your batteries."

Mason got in the car and saw Evie running around to climb in. "He's right," she said as she buckled up. "I mean, I'll follow you to the ends of the earth whether you want me to or not. But you need to slow down from time to time—think things through."

"You really think so?"

"Sure."

Mason rubbed his eyes. "Good, then you can follow me to the hospital. I'll take the day off when I've stopped this maniac." With that, he revved the car to life and sped toward the hospital to question the nine-year-old killer.

CHAPTER SIXTY-TWO

Night had fallen by the time Ryan Carter opened his eyes. They were wandering, lost, looking around as if to identify his surroundings. When asked if he was prepared to talk, he stared with vacant eyes before giving a shallow nod of the head.

Mason led with the simple questions while Bill and Owen stood quietly at the back of the room. The deal was that he could get whatever he needed from the boy before the police swooped in with their special brand of questioning.

"How are you feeling?" Mason asked, settling him gently.

A quick adjustment and a wince. "It hurts."

"That will pass. Ryan, I need you to tell me everything you can, all right?"

The boy nodded.

"Did you speak with the killer?"

"Yes."

Mason removed a sweet picture of Thea Peters, the girl who'd been hanged from the curtain pole only one day earlier. "Do you recognize this girl?"

The heart rate monitor beeped as if it to shout, *objection!*

Ryan's lips moved without a sound, his eyes filling with tears as he shook his head. "Sorry."

"Listen to me, Ryan. You're not in any trouble, but you need to tell us what happened."

A pause, then a wet sniff. "He made me do it."

The boy couldn't have been talking about hanging the girl—there was no way a nine-year-old boy had the strength to haul her up that high, especially if she'd been resisting. It was the writing on the wall that Mason was accusing him of.

"What did he make you do, Ryan?"

Ryan's eyes rolled up as if remembering something he didn't want to. "Often through my curtains peep," he said. "Often through my curtains peep."

Mason's eyes went to the kid's hand that lacked a pinkie. *How could he do this to such an innocent kid?* "It's okay, Ryan. Calm down. What can you tell me about the killer? Did he say where he was going?"

"No." Ryan rolled his head away.

"Did he say what his plans were?"

"No."

"What about the next victim? Has he chosen yet?"

"I don't know!" Ryan screamed a shrill, piercing shriek. "I don't know! I don't know! Just leave me alone!"

Owen Carter came lunging forward to cradle his son, who was thrashing in protest. The heart rate monitor was beeping off the charts, and the bed shook like it was possessed.

Mason went to the back of the room, out the way. *I pushed him too far.*

"You'd better leave, Mr. Black," Owen said. "Thank you for your help, but he's had enough." He shot Mason a cold look, but Mason didn't blame him.

"We're putting surveillance on your house for the next week," Bill told Owen while holding the door for Mason. "If you need anything more from us, you let me know."

Outside the room, where nurses passed every couple of seconds in heavy hospital traffic, Bill patted Mason on the back. "It's not your fault."

"I know."

"You look pretty drained," Evie said, getting up from a chair in the corridor. "Will you please go home and get some sleep? I know you're determined—you have nothing to prove there—but you're useless unless your eyes are wide open."

I guess she has a point. Mason tried to think of a way he could accept defeat with grace. He turned and headed for the exit. "I'll see you both tomorrow."

"Swing by in the morning," Evie called after him.

Mason gave a thumbs-up but didn't turn back. Sure, he could go home and try and sleep it off, but he had a strong suspicion the horrifying look on Ryan's face would haunt him all night long. Desperate to avoid a night of agitated tossing and turning, he went to the Mustang, knowing that the next stop of the night was not his last.

CHAPTER SIXTY-THREE

Rather than heading to Bill's, Mason had dared to go to his own home, stopping to grab a cheap bouquet of flowers on the way. Sandra would think he wanted something from her, but he just wanted to familiarize himself with the only life he'd known for the past decade.

Now he stood at the front door, unwilling to use his key—mostly dreading she'd changed the locks. With a steady knock and a glance at his Rolex, Mason stood waiting.

Eventually, the door popped open. Mason pushed the flowers into Sandra's chest and let himself in, heading straight to the kitchen to pour himself a drink.

Sandra caught up to him. "Sure, invite yourself in," she said.

"I just came to talk. You owe me that." The Jack Daniels spilled into the tumbler as he cleared his throat and prepared himself for the first satisfying gulp.

"Because you got me flowers? They can't buy me back."

"I'm not trying to buy you back. Just... ease off the throttle, will you?"

Sandra drew a deep breath and looked away. "You're right. I'm sorry. Thank you for the flowers." She went to the cupboard to fetch a vase.

Just then, Joshua walked into the room, looking like a deer in headlights. "What're you doing here?" he said after composing himself. "Get out of our house."

Mason felt his cheeks burn up, but there were bigger things than Joshua right now. He hid his clenched fists under the counter. *My house, you prick! My house!*

"It's okay," Sandra said, cutting the hostility out off Joshua's glare. "We're only talking. Just go upstairs. I'll be up when I'm ready."

Glaring at Mason for a few more seconds—the fear in his eyes was impossible to disguise—Joshua left the kitchen and stomped up the stairs, his footsteps echoing through the house.

"Wait. Did you tie his shoelaces?" Mason asked, grinning.

"Don't, Mason. Come on, tell me about the case."

They both took a seat at the island, sharing a drink as he filled her in on everything that had happened so far. For a few minutes, it felt as if he was home again, and his wife was there to hear about his workday. Over the years, she'd been his unofficial shrink. Now, even if just for a momentary lapse, she had resumed the role.

"I really hope you catch him soon," she said. "You deserve that peace."

Mason stared into his near-empty glass. "Thanks. So, change of subject: do you think I could take Amy to see a movie tomorrow night? It'd be good to spend some time with her, with all this going on."

Sandra nodded slowly, as if realizing she didn't mind that much. "Sure. She's in bed, so I'll ask her in the morning, but I'm sure she'd love to." A smile followed, albeit a small one.

Just ask what you want to ask, the nagging voice in Mason's head told him. "Sandra?"

"Uh-huh?"

"About us—"

"Don't do that," she said.

"Do what?"

"Don't ruin a good moment."

"How can I not? I just want to know if this is what you really want." Mason wasn't even sure if he *wanted* her back, but when a ship sprung a leak, your reactions told you to repair it. You never even stop to ponder whether it's worth saving.

Sandra pushed back the kitchen stool and moved to a drawer. She pulled out a brown envelope and slid it across the counter.

"What's this?"

"Divorce papers. I was going to wait until you'd closed your case, but... you know."

"Oh, well thank you *so* much for being the mature one in all this." Mason felt that rage burning up his insides again. He wanted to scream, throw things, maybe even march upstairs and beat the living shit out of Joshua.

But a soft, delicate voice from behind soothed him in a heartbeat.

"Dad?"

Mason turned to see Amy standing in the doorway.

She ran to him, hugging his waist. She'd washed off her makeup, and she'd dyed her hair back to its original color. Even her pajamas were cutesy. It was like she'd been restored to her former self. "I missed you."

"I missed you too, sweetheart. Hey, wanna go see a movie tomorrow?"

"Can it be that new vampire movie?" she asked, beaming.

"Whatever that is, sure." He mussed her hair like he used to do when she was five years old. "I'll pick you up at nine." Now the brown envelope no longer seemed important, and it was only then Mason realized the sole reason he'd been happy with his family was because of Amy. Sandra had little, perhaps nothing, to do with it.

For the next hour they sat and talked about school, and even Sandra laughed a little. For that one hour, they were a family again, and Mason didn't even think about the Lullaby Killer until he left the house.

Now, he thought as he got back in his car and waved to Amy, who stood watching from her bedroom window...

Now to find Marvin Wendell.

CHAPTER SIXTY-FOUR

Evie Black started the new day with research.

Last night's events had already leaked to the press. As promised, she'd had nothing to do with it, so found herself only reading the rival sites, most of them filled with details about how private investigator Mason Black had found the Carter twin. Thankfully, Evie wasn't mentioned, but she still read with pride that her brother was well respected. She'd always hoped—not quite expected, but hoped—he would grow up to be something of a success. After what had happened to their parents, any kind of motivation should have been hard to come by. But Mason seemed to have managed, and managed well.

Crime Online had little to say about the details of the case, as they had a habit of being vague rather than filling in the blanks with their imagination. *First Cut*, on the other hand, had much more to express, including an interview with one Vincent Romero.

Drawn in by the headline—*FRIEND OF LULLABY KILLER SPEAKS OUT*—Evie clicked and watched the interview. She hadn't known him by name, but he was the clerk of the motel and claimed he'd been friends with the killer for a couple of years.

The video showed Romero, who seemed to be trying not to grin.

"I didn't know his real name or that he was a killer," he told the camera in a fake display of shame. *"I only knew he was a press researcher, kind of quiet and a little strange."* His whole performance was probably just to draw attention to his business. The world was full of attention-seeking con artists, and Evie was sick of them.

Reaching for her phone, she found Mason's number and dialed.

"Hey, Evie."

"The clerk lied to us."

"What?" Mason sounded as if he was still waking up.

"He was interviewed for a news channel. Says he had dinners with the killer, drinks with him after work some nights. This has been going on for..." Evie scrolled through the page. "... a couple years, apparently."

"Wait, what? Slow down." Mason grunted, as if was just getting out of bed. "He said he didn't know the guy."

"Well, now he says otherwise."

"Could he be glory-seeking?"

"Maybe," Evie said, walking around the room and filling her purse with things she might need for the day. "But wouldn't you like to know for sure?"

Mason huffed, clearing his throat. "Right. You coming?"

"You bet your ass I am."

CHAPTER SIXTY-FIVE

Mason picked her up in a hurry. This time he was driving, and he wasn't holding back. Flooring it, they tore up the road and got there in no time, climbed out, and stormed toward the clerk's office.

"Already open for business," Evie said, pointing at the motel room where they'd recovered Ryan Carter only yesterday. "Makes you sick, doesn't it?"

Mason shook his head in disbelief and burst into the office. "I have a bone to pick with you," he said as he barged between two customers at the counter. He was vaguely aware of Evie behind him, showing the customers out and making them aware of the recent murders on site.

"What the hell do you want?"

"I want to know why you lied to us."

Romero sat down behind the counter, made a *pfft* noise, and turned away from them. "What're you talking about?"

"You said you'd only exchanged a few words with Wendell." Mason realized the clerk didn't know the name, so corrected himself to what had been signed in the ledger. "Brahm, I mean. Now you're telling the press you were friends. You'd better start telling some goddamn truths. I've come too far for you to be tripping me up."

"Whatever." The clerked waved a hand. "That was just to increase business."

Evie stepped forward. "You said you knew he was a press researcher. How could you have possibly known that?"

Romero looked at her, moving his mouth like he was searching for an answer. "Go fuck yourself, little girl."

Something inside Mason snapped. Without thinking he lunged over the counter and grabbed the man's tie. With his other hand, he reached for the nearby stapler, dragged Romero closer, and whacked a staple into the desk beside his cheek.

The man cried out in terror. "You crazy shit!"

"I'm going to get a whole lot crazier if you don't stop fucking with us."

"All right!" He put his hands up, shaking. "All right. He brings whores here, okay? I-I didn't want to say anything because I don't want the police to find out."

"We knew about the whores." Mason dragged him closer. "What we want to know is *why here*?"

"What do you mean? He needs somewhere private."

"But why here, especially? You're miles out of town. There're hundreds of places to stay before you reach this shithole dive." Mason saw Evie fingering through some paperwork from the counter, totally relaxed.

"For God's sake," Romero cried. "I offer him discounts for continued use. He can't do it at home. His m-mother wouldn't approve. Now let me go!"

Mason tightened his grip, pulling him farther over the counter. "The killer doesn't live with his mom."

"Yes he does!" Romero cried. "I swear!"

Mason thought back to when they'd met Mrs. Wendell, and to how relaxed and unconcerned she'd been. Now it'd been brought to his attention, she *had* seemed unsurprised. As if she knew about him. As if she were protecting him.

"If you're lying, I'll be back. Evie?" Mason pushed the owner back into his chair, almost toppling it. He straightened himself out, dusting off the sleeves of his trench coat.

"Yep?"

"Let's go."

CHAPTER SIXTY-SIX

Mason killed the engine and reached into the glove compartment for the revolver.

"And what exactly do you plan to do with that?" Evie asked, pushing her glasses up her nose. She'd never liked guns. Not since a sex-obsessed creep had tried his luck raping her a few years ago. Lucky for her, Mason had been there to disarm the guy. Even broke his nose in the process. And three fingers.

"I'm not doing anything with it. It's for you." Mason checked the cylinder and dumped it in her hand. "If I'm not back in exactly ten minutes—"

"You're not going in there unarmed?"

"I'm not leaving *you* unarmed. I'll take my chances."

"Mason—" Evie tried, but by then he'd already shut the door on her.

He looked up the street and stalked toward the house.

In all honesty, he had no idea what might happen

when he spoke to Mrs. Wendell. If she was going to insist that her son—Marvin—didn't still live here, he would have to leave and return later with the police and their search warrants.

Mason tried the door and waited, listening close for any signs of someone being home. Not a peep. *Something isn't right here.* Careful and quiet, he snuck around the side of the house and spotted an open window. Looking both ways, he pried it open and hustled through.

A soft thud as he landed announced his presence to the household. He could hear a TV now, coming from another room. Some shouting from a talk show about who the father might be. But if the TV was on, Mason assumed someone was home to watch it.

He gently pushed open the door that led into the living room. The last time he was here, he'd been an invited guest. Now he felt less than welcome. Still, the job needed doing, so he pressed his back to the wall and crept into the living room, watching his corners.

By the time he saw the shotgun's barrel in his face, it was too late.

"You shouldn't have come back here," said a red-faced Mrs. Wendell.

Mason took a step back, raising his hands. "Put the gun down."

Mrs. Wendell looked miniscule behind the heavy, double-barreled shotgun. Small but dangerous. She twitched the end, directing him to the couch. "I won't let you take my boy away. They already took my baby girl, but they won't get their hands on my boy."

Mason sat on the couch, careful not to make any sudden movements as his heart danced inside his chest. "I'm doing what has to be done. Your son is a killer, Mrs. Wendell. Protecting him will only get more children murdered. That blood will be on *your* hands, too."

She lowered her eyes—but not the weapon—for a fleeting moment. "That doesn't make it okay. I can't be alone in this world. I won't."

Despite having to choose his words with care, Mason led with his emotions. "I don't give a rat's ass if you're alone. Don't you think there are more important things than your loneliness? Not two days ago, I had to look at an eight-year-old girl dangling from a curtain pole. Your son is a monster, and he needs to go to prison."

Mrs. Wendell shook her head, refusing to let a single word sink in. "No," she said. "You can't take him. You won't."

"Then I'll have to come back with the strength of the SFPD behind me."

The woman stepped back too fast for it not to look aggressive. She tightened her grip on the gun. "You're not leaving here, Mr. Black. I'm sorry, but you can't."

CHAPTER SIXTY-SEVEN

Your ten minutes are up.

Evie had every right to panic. When Mason had said, *"if I'm not back in ten minutes,"* she'd assumed he was making a dry and cliché joke. But those minutes slogged by while she held the revolver, and now she had to take action.

She left the car and skirted around the house, where she'd seen Mason stalk out of view not long ago. She found an open window, and she peered through.

If anything has happened to him, she thought, *I'll never forgive myself.*

Stowing the revolver in her pocket, she climbed through the window, nimble as a cat. Only as she landed, her elbow caught on something solid, knocking it to the floor. Whatever it was shattered, and Evie winced while her heart stopped for a flicker of a moment.

Seeing the blinking lights of the TV in the next room

and praying she hadn't been heard, Evie pulled out the revolver once more and crept around the door.

When she saw her brother, she gasped.

Mason was sitting on the couch, talking.

Mrs. Wendell, who was threatening him with a shotgun, had her back to Evie and hadn't noticed her arrival. Desperate not to make a sound, Evie crept up behind her and placed the revolver against the back of the woman's head.

"Drop the gun," she said, knowing damn well she couldn't shoot another human being.

"Goddamnit." Mrs. Wendell let the gun slip from her hand and fall to the ground.

Evie walked around to her brother's side. "You okay, Mase?"

"All good, if only you'd stop calling me *Mase*." He rose and took the shotgun from beside Mrs. Wendell. Although he'd had an angry old woman threatening to blast his face into pieces, he seemed totally unfazed. Unlike Evie, whose hands still shook from the tension.

"What's the betting you don't have a permit for this?" Mason smirked at Mrs. Wendell. "You can drop the gun now, Evie."

Evie sighed with relief as she handed the revolver to Mason, thankful to have the thing out of her hands. "Should we call the police? Bill? Anyone?"

"Not yet," Mason said. "First, Mrs. Wendell is going to show us to her son's bedroom."

Mrs. Wendell pulled a disgusted face, as if they had no right to be there. "I will not."

"I wasn't asking." Mason aimed the revolver at her forehead.

CHAPTER SIXTY-EIGHT

Between fantasies of slicing off another child's finger and looking at Mason Black's expression as he realized he should have stayed away, Marvin Wendell turned the corner and spotted the car at once.

For God's sake!

All he'd asked for was a little time to go home and collect some things, and then he could hit the road, making only one stop along the way. Now, the game had changed.

Now, he was done making threats.

Evie Black was running from the car, a pistol of some kind gripped in her hands. She was heading toward the Wendells' house. Toward his *home*. Stopping him from having fun was one thing, but intruding on his privacy? Well, that was another issue entirely.

What were they doing in there? Harassing his mother? The thought made him sick. She was such a lovely woman, deep down. Sure, she'd had trouble showing it, always putting him down and making him feel as though he wasn't good enough. But she was his mother, for crying out loud, and he loved her.

Wendell waited until Evie was out of sight, then drove the RV past the house. Now he had nowhere to go; the motel had been compromised, and it seemed as though his home was out of bounds. By now, he could have had a million dollars and been hitting the road, killing wherever—and whenever—he pleased.

Marvin had a new destination in mind, and he made his way there, grinding his teeth and trying not to scream with rage. *Two can play at that game*, he thought as he passed the parked Mustang.

He would be diverting from his original plan, but he could still cause some real drama for the PI. It was like severing a limb with a butter knife: messy, but not impossible.

With a smile on his face and his foot on the pedal, he headed toward Mason's home.

CHAPTER SIXTY-NINE

They were led into a dirty attic room, and the sight was astounding.

Photographs lined the walls, pinned up with thumbtacks and tape, every wall a collage of sentimental photography. A computer sat in the corner—multiple screens, all lit up with background usage.

Mason dragged Mrs. Wendell to the bed and pushed her onto it. "Sit, and don't say a word." He then joined Evie at the computer as she clicked through a series of open windows. "What do you have?"

"Everything," Evie said, typing away. She brought up an opened email inbox, saw her name, and clicked into the messages. "It's them. This was him."

"Brahm?" Mason had expected as much. "Amelia is safe, right?"

Evie nodded and Mason approached the wall. Some of the pictures were disturbing, showing cut-up corpses. But others were more dignified. Some were of Mason, but not as he was now. They'd been taken back when he was with the SFPD, showing him walking away from the Lullaby Killer's first crime scene. Mason recognized the look of torment on his own face. It was the day he'd lost faith in humanity.

"You look younger there," Evie said, coming over to examine the pictures. She held her hand over her mouth in astonishment as she saw some of the more gruesome ones. "At least we know this Wendell guy is the killer."

"Was there ever any doubt?"

"No, but now we know he's not a copycat. Besides, this is concrete proof."

Mason continued along the wall. Missy Daniels had been photographed a lot. There were no photos of the twins, which seemed strange. His attention was drawn to a young, blonde-haired girl sitting under a tree with her friends. "Who's that?"

"That's Amelia," Evie said, alarmed.

"Wow." Mason hadn't seen her since she was a baby and hadn't seen any photos since she'd turned seven. He often wondered what she would be like now, and whether she'd get along with Amy. "She's beautiful."

Evie gave a thin smile, wiped her eye, and moved on.

"My son has never done anything wrong," Mrs. Wendell protested. "He's a good boy. So what if he likes to take photographs? There's no harm in that."

"Your son is sick and demented," Mason said, moving to a nearby refrigerator. "Now, shut up. I won't tell you again." Keen to uncover more of the man's secrets, he opened the refrigerator door and stood back in shock.

It was like the air had been knocked from his chest.

"What is it?" Evie asked, coming to see for herself. When she saw it, she gagged and turned away, retching noisily.

"Evie," Mason said, still horrified, his hate for Wendell doubling. He stared with disgust at the jar of severed fingers. "Call it in."

CHAPTER SEVENTY

Officers and the forensics team swarmed the house. Other bits and pieces had been found, trophies of the murdered children.

"You know," Mason said, pulling Evie out of an officer's way. The air was thick, and it was becoming tough to breathe inside. "If Amelia is safe, maybe you should get an exclusive on this. Give your career the kick start it needs."

Evie sighed. "I do miss the lifestyle, but I don't have the energy for it just yet."

"Why not? You're the first one on the scene. People will worship you."

While Evie seemed to consider it, Captain Cox came into the room. "No," she said, and had obviously been eavesdropping. "This doesn't get out yet. We're setting up an ambush team across the street."

"You think he'll be back?" Mason asked.

"Maybe. You're welcome to stick around and find out."

Mason looked around him. Mrs. Wendell was being escorted out in handcuffs and would probably be charged with obstruction of justice. The photographs and computer were being taken as evidence, for all the good it would do. There must have been a lot of personal attachment to this house, so maybe Marvin Wendell would come back. But Mason didn't need to be there to see it—as much as he wanted to.

"Afraid not," he said. "I have somewhere to be." Nine o'clock was fast approaching, so he would soon be taking Amy to see that movie. He didn't care if the film turned out to be a flop, as long as he got to spend time with his daughter.

"Can I get a ride?" Evie rubbed her eyes, the dark patches covered only for a second by her knuckles. "I need a drink. Or something."

"Sure." Mason led her out to the car, with every intention of leaving the crime scene behind him. But try as he might, it was unlikely he would shake the horrendous image of the finger jar from his mind.

CHAPTER SEVENTY-ONE

Sandra brushed her hair as she stared at the reflection of Joshua in the mirror.

"I just don't see why you had to let him in, is all," Joshua complained.

"It is his house, you know." Sandra slammed down the brush and went over to sit on the bed. She was fidgeting again, clearing things off the bedside table and rummaging through the drawers. It was mostly to delay joining him.

"Not for much longer," Joshua said, his eyes not leaving his book on stamina increase.

This was the thing that got to her; although at first he'd just been her Pilates instructor, they'd become closer with each session. Sandra's relationship to Mason had been on the rocks anyway, so why shouldn't she have sought comfort in the arms of another? When their cheap little affair turned into something more emotional, she started learning more things about him.

Some of those things were bad. For instance, he was a coward.

"You stole the man's wife and moved in with his family," she said matter-of-factly, slamming the drawer closed and joining him on the bed. "You have to expect some sort of reaction from him."

Joshua made an incoherent noise. It seemed like he was about to say something, when a frantic pounding on the bedroom door silenced him.

"Mom, open up. Something's wrong."

Sandra clambered out of bed and rushed across the room, stealing a quick glance at the clock. They'd hoped to get an early night with Amy heading out to meet her father.

But that didn't seem likely now.

When she opened the door, Amy looked like a frightened mess. Her skin was a ghostly white, and she shook as she whispered, "There's someone at the window."

Skeptical and worn-out, Sandra studied her. "What are you talking about?"

"My bedroom window. I was getting ready to see Dad and heard something outside. I went to the window, and there was a man—"

"For God's sake, Amy. It's dark outside. The mind plays all sorts of tricks on our eyes, especially when you're looking at shadows." Exhausted, Sandra closed the door on her. It seemed like one thing after the other tonight.

Who else wants to piss me off?

Convinced she wouldn't be able to sleep tonight—she

was far too angry for that—she climbed into bed, turned off her lamp, and did her best to ignore Joshua's huffing judgment.

The minutes crawled by, and she was barely into a light sleep, when a high-pitched scream pierced the air. Sandra froze.

"What the..." Her words trailed off as she leapt out of bed and threw a robe around herself. Joshua was waking up too slow. Sandra wouldn't wait for him.

She ran to Amy's room, panicking that she'd dismissed her cries for help as she stumbled across the landing in the dark and pushed open Amy's bedroom door.

A dark figure stood lurking in the black of the room. He wore a long coat, and his arm was hooked around Amy's throat. The gun in his hand was aimed at Sandra, while her daughter kicked her legs out, struggling for breath.

"Mrs. Black," the man said. The excitement in his voice rose the hairs on the back of her neck. "How nice to finally meet ya." He threw his head back as he let out a laugh.

A chill ran up Sandra's spine, and she involuntarily shivered as she understood who this man was and why he was here.

And that she probably wouldn't survive the night.

CHAPTER SEVENTY-TWO

The Lullaby Killer stared at Joshua as he came bounding into the room wearing nothing but a pair of boxer shorts and a T-shirt. "Who are you, the replacement? Hah. You're a lot smaller than Mr. Black, aren't you? Speaking of which, will he be joining us?"

Joshua said nothing and pressed his back against the wall.

"He'll be here any minute." Sandra saw no point in lying. Sickened by Joshua's cowardice, she hoped Mason would burst in here to save the day with all guns blazing. But that wasn't her luck. It'd *never* been her luck.

The killer herded them downstairs and into the dark living room and ordered them to sit on the couch, but his arm remained firm around Amy's neck, the gun still held at her temple as her face turned red.

"We'd better get a move on, then, hey?" The killer pulled her back and kept the gun trained on Sandra. "Where do you keep your tools?"

What does he need tools for? "In the garage."

"And zip ties?"

"We don't have any." It was a lie. Sandra suspected what he wanted them for.

The killer sighed. "You couldn't lie to save your life, could you? Look, there are two ways to keep you still. The other is a little more permanent. So, I'll ask again... are there any zip ties in your garage?"

Sandra hesitated, then finally gave in. "Yes."

"Okay." The killer shoved Amy forward, sending her crashing to her knees. "You go get them. But no funny business. If you're not back in sixty seconds with those ties, you can kiss goodbye to Mommy and her new squeeze."

Amy stopped, frightened. Tears sparkled in her eyes.

"Fifty-nine, fifty-eight," the killer taunted.

It was enough to get her on her feet and scurrying out of the room.

"What do you want from us?" Sandra asked, ashamed Joshua had yet to utter a single word of defense or protest. *Some man.*

"Oh, don't be so goddamn naive. You know what I want."

The sixty seconds ticked by with the gun aimed at her, and Amy returned with what the psychopath had demanded. She handed them over and moved to sit with her mother but was stopped short.

"Nuh-uh." The killer tossed the bag of zip ties to Sandra and beckoned Amy with his finger. "Get over here and let Mommy get to work."

"Please," Sandra begged, sniffling, "let her go and I'll do what you want."

"You'll do what I want whether you like it or not. Now, don't make me ask again."

Amy shuffled back toward him.

"Tie yourselves."

"What?" Joshua said, his voice cracking.

"You heard me. Hands behind your backs, and zip your wrists."

Sandra hesitated and mumbled to Joshua that they should do as they were told; then they helped each other tie their hands. When they were done, the killer stepped forward and attached their ties together, back-to-back.

"This girl is mine now," the Lullaby Killer said.

"Please..." Sandra began.

"Shh. Go with a little dignity, woman." He took a cell phone from his pocket and placed it by her feet. "If you want a shot at getting her back, make sure Mr. Black gets this." He raised the pistol to his shoulder and walloped Joshua with the butt of the gun, knocking him unconscious.

Amy yelped in shock, while Sandra flinched and screwed shut her eyes.

The killer dragged Amy with him, leaving Sandra subdued, afraid, and wondering how long it would be before Mason arrived and if she would ever see their daughter again.

CHAPTER SEVENTY-THREE

Mason pulled up outside Evie's, anxious to get going.

"You'd better get some rest," she said as she opened the car door.

"Can't. I'm taking Amy to a movie."

"Ah, right. Plans. Well, enjoy yourself and keep me updated on the case." Evie got out, closed the door, and went toward her apartment.

Should I... Mason sat gnawing on his knuckles, unsure if it was a smart move. Then, before it was too late, he opened the window and called after her. "Come with us."

Evie stopped and turned. "What?"

"Come with us. She's your niece, after all."

It was the biggest smile he'd seen from her in years as she headed back to the Mustang.

Mason didn't want to be late. He didn't want to do anything to disappoint his daughter, so he sped back to the house while ignoring Evie's complaints that he was going too fast. From his point of view there was no such thing as *too fast*. Not when Amy was waiting on the other end.

When they pulled into the drive, something—although Mason couldn't tell what just yet—wasn't quite right. He sensed inactivity in the house, and none of the lights were on. Then he spotted the front door ajar.

"So, I'm thinking maybe a subtle job." Evie droned on about her potential plans for the next year. "Just movie reviews or restaurant critiquing, you know?"

But Mason wasn't listening to a word. He had that feeling in his stomach—the one that told him he couldn't relax. "Hand me that revolver."

"What?" Evie pulled a face.

"The gun. Now." He took it from her and exited the car, heading up the drive like he'd been taught at the academy. It was second nature to him now, creaking open the door, waving a hand to draw a warning gunshot from an overambitious shooter before heading inside with the barrel raised and his back to each wall. He started in the living room and was shocked by what he saw.

"Mason?" Sandra called out to him in the dimly lit room.

"What the hell?" He rushed to her, kneeled by her side, and examined the binds. "What happened? Where's Amy?"

"She's gone..."

Mason didn't hear that last part. Or rather he did but didn't *want* to. He took the stairs two at a time, despite his huge size. "Amy!" he called, grimly imagining what he might find. "Amy!"

At the end of the corridor, he burst into her room, raising the gun once more. He was expecting to find something sinister, something dangerous. Instead, all that remained were the drapes blowing in the wind, reaching out toward an empty room where his daughter was suppose to sleep—where she was supposed to be safe.

Mason felt a knot in his stomach. He knew he'd messed up, knew there was no coming back from this one. Even if he were to get Amy back safely, he would never be able to forgive himself for not being there.

CHAPTER SEVENTY-FOUR

Mason trudged downstairs, his soul in pieces and his head a wreck. *Why didn't I just stay away like Sandra told me? Time after time, she told me!*

It was clear to him now: his loyalty to the job had grown far too strong for him to handle. Now it was affecting his personal life, and it was nothing more than punishment.

Evie was cutting the zip ties off Sandra and Joshua as he came back into the living room.

"Are you all right?" he asked Sandra, fighting the urge to punch something. His eyes went to Joshua, who was climbing to his feet without a word. Mason lunged forward and grabbed him by his throat, pinning him down on the couch. "You were supposed to be protecting them, you piece of shit!"

"Mason, come on," Evie pleaded from behind.

"If you make a man's family your own, the least you can do is make sure they're fucking safe!" Mason raised his fist, and it took everything he had not to pummel the guy. On any normal day, he'd have relished the sight of this coward's blood on his fists, but right now, he was incomplete—broken.

"It's not worth it." Evie pressed her palm against his fist, encouraging him to lower it. "He's not worth it."

Mason lowered his arm. But not his gaze, staring daggers at Joshua as he stepped back. "I want Bill here," he said matter-of-factly. "His best team, everything they have to get my little girl back."

"I'm on it." Evie pulled out her phone and left the room, pressing it to her ear.

"Mason." Sandra stepped to his side.

"Not now." His life was collapsing around him. Was this his fault?

"It's important."

"Not now! I—" He turned to see the phone held out to him and glared at it.

"That creep told me to make sure you get this." Sandra handed it to him, and it beeped as soon as he took it.

It was a text message from a phonebook entry named *Brahm*. Mason stared at it for a long time, not wanting to read it. What if it was a photograph of Amy? What if it was a short, snappy sentence to confirm he'd killed her? Or worse.

Finally, taking everything he had, he read the message. As he did, he was knocked back by those three fate-sealing words.

"What does it say?" Sandra begged, her lips quivering in fear.

Mason couldn't speak. He handed her the phone and slouched back into the armchair. He watched her expression as she read, moving her lips to the words that would play over and over in his mind until the day he died.

Hush, little baby.

CHAPTER SEVENTY-FIVE

Sandra handed the phone back, horrified.

Some weeks ago, Mason would have been the one to comfort her. Instead, he watched her hand come to her face as she gasped into her own palm and fought hard not to cry. Joshua did nothing, Mason noticed while he stared at the text and considered his options.

Another text came through, and a third in quick succession.

I'm not sure I want to read these.

But he had to.

Expecting the worst, he opened them and read aloud. *"She belongs to me now."* It felt disgusting. Perverted. And that was just the first one. *"Would she really miss this finger?"*

For a few minutes they sat, waiting for the police to turn up. When they did, they were interviewed and questioned, and prints were taken off every surface the killer had touched.

Even Bill looked to be in shock as he comforted his old friend.

"Please, help me," Mason said to him, swallowing his pride. "I know I let you down before. I know your son died because I couldn't stop this guy. But please, just... help me."

Bill stood assessing him. And who could blame him? It was a Mason Black he'd never seen before. "I'll do what I can. But I wouldn't know where to start."

"So, that's the extent of the SFPD's help? It's all well and good that I was consulted, but I thought you guys might have something to go by." Mason went to the wall and put his face in his hands. "I'm sorry."

"You don't have to be."

Mason had no idea what to do. How could he help his little girl? Why did the killer leave the cell phone, if only to taunt him? Just as he asked himself these questions, the phone rang on the table with an eerie circus theme.

"Shut up. Everyone shut up!" Bill yelled, and the room fell silent.

Mason went to the table and reached for the cell phone with one trembling hand. The screen read *Brahm*. A cruel jest. An inside joke. A sick sense of humor.

Knowing he would regret it, Mason answered.

"Hello?"

"Mr. Black, how nice to hear from you. You're doing all right, I hope?" The killer's voice sounded odd, his relaxed tone very unlike his mother's. Something about it gave Mason the sense he'd truly fallen off the sanity wagon.

Mason put the phone on speaker and sat it on the table. "Keep your filthy fucking hands away from my daughter. You hear me?"

"Aw, don't be like that. Stay positive and you might be able to help her."

That must mean she's still alive. Mason looked at Bill, who was taking notes and snapping his fingers at a nearby techie. It looked like he was trying to get the call traced, but Mason knew they wouldn't get time. "What do you want?"

"You."

There was a dreadful silence, but it spoke volumes. Evie stood at the back of the room and nibbled on her nails.

"Why?"

"Because you're a pain in the ass. So, I'm gonna offer you a deal. Your life in exchange for hers." There was a long pause. "What do you say?"

Mason didn't even have to think about it. The only question was whether the killer would stay loyal to his proposal. Somehow, Mason didn't think so. "You're bluffing."

Marvin Wendell laughed. "Only one way to find out, huh? You have exactly ten minutes to get to Cliffside Hill. A second later, she dies. Come alone, or she dies. The clock's ticking, Mr. Black."

Mason knew the place—you couldn't go any farther before you plummeted to the rocks below. It was a common place for teenagers to hang out, but never late at night.

"I'll be waiting," Wendell said.

The call ended, and Mason stuffed the phone into his pocket.

"What're you going to do?" Evie asked, still chewing the polish from her nails.

But Mason didn't hear her.

He was already halfway out the door.

CHAPTER SEVENTY-SIX

Amy had tried banging and screaming, but it was hopeless. Nobody was around to help her, and even if they were, they wouldn't be able to hear her. The killer had made her well aware of that when he'd slid open the mailbox-sized slot.

"It's soundproof," he'd said. "Try all you want, but nobody will hear you."

With this in mind, she became silent in the darkness. The cool metal pressed against her cheek, while her eyes were sore with streams of hot, stinging tears. She would let them out now, while the killer wasn't looking—her father had taught her to be strong, so that was the only side of herself she would let show.

As much as she wanted to beg for her life, Amy sat in silence. If she could just get a moment to talk with the man, she might be able to manipulate him a little. So total silence was probably her best bet.

After a while, he must have noticed she'd been mute.

He opened up the slide and peered through, looking over his shoulder instead of at the road.

"Where are you taking me?" Amy asked, leveling her voice to sound calm.

The killer crooked an eyebrow and closed the slide, inviting darkness.

Amy was left alone again, if only for a few seconds.

The slide came open once more. "Away."

She knew he hadn't been taking her home. Why would he? He had everything he'd ever wanted now, and even her father might not be able to stop him.

But that didn't keep her from praying.

CHAPTER SEVENTY-SEVEN

Mason blasted through the dark with nothing but the Mustang's headlights to guide him.

Cliffside Hill. That was where he had to go. It was lucky he knew the place. He'd taken Sandra to the restaurant for their proposal dinner all those years ago. Mason didn't think the killer knew that, so it was a hell of a coincidence.

The cell phone jingled in his lap.

Another text.

Mason steered with one hand and read it with the other: *Time is running out.*

He was damn right about that. With only four minutes left on the clock, he had to punch the gas. Maybe he could make it if he cut a corner or two, but this would have to be the best driving of his life.

He eased on the brake and swung the rear end of the Mustang around the bend. It was a heavy machine, not built for this kind of precision driving. It roared as it gripped the road, belching out smoke from beneath the screeching tires.

Not far to go.

The phone went off again. A picture of Amy. She was crying now, sending Mason into a blind rage. *Nobody lays a hand on my little girl.* By the looks of it, she had a cliff and the moonlit sky not far behind her. There was another message attached.

Two minutes.

Mason couldn't check his phone again. Every second was vital.

With the clock ticking and his adrenaline at an all-time high, he pushed the car to its limit and pierced through the darkness.

CHAPTER SEVENTY-EIGHT

The wind howled as spatters of rain assaulted his face, numbing his cheeks and ears. It was unbearably cold, but worth it just to prove a point.

"Sit quiet," Wendell said, setting up his climactic display. Nothing had ever been more exhilarating than this. Sure, he'd hurt and killed the real little shits. This girl didn't seem like one of them. She seemed smart but not enough to grow up and become a bitchy manipulator. A tease. She was pretty but didn't seem to know it. She was... normal.

But she still has to die.

The girl was sobbing, too—trying to hide it, but definitely sobbing.

"Stop that stupid noise," he demanded, tightening the rope. It was difficult enough to get ready in time. Mr. Black would soon be at the target location, and he hadn't even finished up here yet.

"My dad will come for me," the girl protested, feigning toughness.

"He'd better." This was everything the killer wanted. This would be the last time anyone tried to fuck with him. *Why did anyone even try to stop me? I was doing a good thing, for crying out loud. Why should these little bastards get to enjoy their childhoods?*

"He's going to kick your ass."

Wendell was losing patience. He went to his tool bag and retrieved the pliers. "I was going to do this last, but since it's the only way to shut you up..." He stepped forward and pulled her from the side of the van. She was surprisingly heavy for a girl her age, and the kicking around didn't help. Halfway to the edge of the cliff, he gave up and hurled her to the rocky ground.

"What are you doing?" she asked, scrambling backward. The tears came again.

"Little girls need to be punished." He lunged forward and grabbed her wrist, forcing her hand into a steady position while she screamed and thrashed, trying to hit him.

She wasn't strong enough to stop him.

"Please!" Desperation laced her screams.

The killer placed the metal ridges on either side of her pinkie finger and squeezed until she cried. He held still, letting the fear and pain linger as he marveled at how much control he had. Never had he felt so powerful, so godlike and in control.

"Ah, you ain't worth it, sweetheart," he said and shoved her into the dirt.

The girl rolled to her side and spewed into a puddle, clutching her hand.

"Now, shut the hell up. I got work to do."

"You're a monster," the girl said, weeping.

"Oh, honey. No, no. I'm the product of a monster." Wendell thought about his home being invaded by Mason Black. "The real criminal is trying to stop me."

CHAPTER SEVENTY-NINE

Bill was driving as fast as he could while Evie kept lookout beside him. "He's getting farther away," he said, shifting gears with a stern look.

"Just do what you can."

They'd jumped into the car as soon as Mason had left the house. Marvin Wendell had told him to come alone, but they couldn't allow it. If only they could hang back and out of view, Amy might remain unharmed. But if Mason was in a tight spot, Evie would never forgive herself for refusing to act.

"We're going to lose him if we don't go faster." Bill protested that they should catch up, but Evie remained firm.

"Stay steady."

Although Bill was right, and they did in fact lose sight of Mason's taillights in the distance, they at least knew they weren't far behind.

They drove farther up the hill, where strong gusts of wind buffeted the car. Evie knew they were near Cliffside now, and they would locate her brother in no time at all. "Switch off your lights."

"What? It's pitch-black out here, are you cra—"

"Just do it." As soon as she spotted the stationary Mustang on the hill, she pointed up at it, which motivated Bill to obey her. "Stop the car." They screeched to a halt and she climbed out, running up the hill in the dark toward Mason's car.

Please be inside, please be inside.

Mason was good at taking care of himself, and Evie wouldn't have to worry there. But when Amy was involved, *someone* was going to get hurt. Evie only hoped it would be the Lullaby Killer.

It took a few minutes to reach the car, trudging uphill against the wind and in the heavy shower. After clawing her way to the top, she could see the door was open and the engine was shut off. Only the dome light lent any illumination to the vacant interior.

"Shit!" she said, getting drenched in the rain. She looked back down the hill, where Bill was watching her from the dry safety of his own car.

Evie turned back around, and a light on the car seat caught her eye. She leaned in, reached for it, and gripped the cell phone in her hand. There was a picture on the screen. It was Amy, and she stood on the edge of the cliff. Her lip was curved in as if she was crying.

"Son of a bitch," Evie muttered.

Mason was lost to her, and Amy was in big trouble. It was clear to her now: in spite of her efforts, the Lullaby Killer was going to win.

CHAPTER EIGHTY

Mason's hands were up in surrender as he stared at the end of the gun.

"Take off your coat," Wendell instructed. "I want to see that gun of yours."

After all these years, it felt surreal to see the infamous Lullaby Killer in the flesh. Mason had expected nothing more than the ordinary-looking man he'd seen in the photographs, but over time he had built up an image of a demon in his mind. Seeing him in person now, standing face-to-face, he did indeed look just like a regular man—save for the missing finger on his left hand.

"If you insist." Mason slid off his trench coat, and it flumped to the wet ground. His black T-shirt was soaked through and clung to his skin. He had to fight not to shiver or show any weakness.

Wendell looked at the revolver in the holster, and his eyes widened. "I'll take that. Damn risky of you, Mr.

Black." Keeping the gun trained on him, Wendell took out the revolver and threw it into the bushes behind him.

While he had his back turned, Mason saw a fleeting opportunity to rush the killer. It was perfectly possible to tackle him and knock the gun from his hand. But if he did that he knew he would never see Amy again. Instead, and with difficulty, he bided his time. "Where is my daughter?"

Wendell offered a sly grin, then nodded at the RV.

"Inside?"

"Go on."

Mason doubted Amy would be tucked away inside the RV, but he couldn't take the risk of not checking. Grunting, he walked toward the door with his hands in the air, still resisting the urge to fight this son of a bitch.

"Open it." The killer waved the pistol around.

With caution, Mason pried open the side door. He hadn't truly expected to see her inside, and it came as no surprise when faced with only the metal backing he'd seen once before.

"Get in."

Mason sighed, lowered his hands, and turned to face the killer. "Why don't you just kill me and let her go? You'll still go free when all is said and done."

"You'd let me go that easily?" He chuckled. "I'm disappointed."

"If it gets my daughter out of harm's way, sure." Mason wondered about the future victims this guy would take. It felt wrong to be sacrificing himself for his daughter, thus letting the elusive Lullaby Killer carry on his nefarious business. "Makes sense, right?"

For a passing moment, Wendell lowered his eyes. It was like he was considering taking Mason's advice. But then a light returned to his expression, and he stepped forward with the gun still trained on Mason. "I need you alive. At least, until that little girl has watched you suffer in agony before your death. After that, maybe I'll give her a swift end. Then again, she seems as if she could take a little torture." Wendell grinned and shoved him toward the door.

Against his better judgment, Mason climbed into the back of the RV, hoping—praying—that he'd be able to get Amy to safety. At any cost.

CHAPTER EIGHTY-ONE

Although Bill was approaching, Evie needed to run. There was just no time to wait for him, no matter how much she needed his help.

Down at the bottom of the slope was the killer's RV. Mason was climbing into it while Marvin Wendell took sanctuary behind the trigger of a gun. It wasn't looking good for her brother *or* her niece, but she had to try to do *something*.

The slope was steep—too steep to make it down unscathed. But as Wendell was closing the side door of the RV, it looked as though timing was everything.

Bill finally caught her up, panting. "Shit, Evie! Where's he taking him?"

Evie peered over the edge, judging her chances. She estimated an 80 percent chance of survival, but only a 2 percent chance of it not hurting like hell.

But I have to try.

Reluctant, she took a deep breath and stepped back.

"What're you doing?" Bill asked, but there was no time to let him talk her out of it.

It was now or never.

Evie took a run-up and threw herself down the slope. She landed on her ass and shuffled her feet, trying to break her descent into a set of smaller falls. The main risk was that if her foot caught, she'd flip over, ending her crazy rescue attempt in a barreling mess of broken bones.

She picked up speed and caught a hazy blur of the killer climbing into the RV. Hopefully he wouldn't see her, and if God was on her side, she would make it in time.

But as the rocks tore at her skin, flipping and rolling her, she heard the hum of the engine below her. The headlights came on, and she was nowhere even close to stopping him.

More debris caught her as she tumbled, tearing up her arms. She was vaguely aware of Bill calling after her. *The idiot is going to give me away.* Evie dug in her heel and managed to slow herself as she approached the bottom of the slope.

And then the RV moved.

No.

Evie was thrown chest-first into the dirt as she hit the bottom. Glancing up, she spotted the ladder on the back of the RV and stumbled forward, turning her combat roll into a dash. She was getting closer.

The RV was moving faster.

She was fifteen feet from reaching the ladder.

Ten feet.

Seven.

Five.

With everything she had left in the tank, Evie darted forward, planted her right foot down, and leapt as far as she could with an outstretched arm. It was a final, desperate grope for the ladder as it moved away.

Please slow down, she thought as it moved out of reach.

CHAPTER EIGHTY-TWO

Mason felt the cold discomfort of the steel and wondered how many children had been kept here before meeting their grisly, premature end. How many had been locked away, scared and alone? How many of them knew they were going to die, and how many cried? The thoughts disgusted him as the RV traveled, with any luck, toward Amy.

Finally, a rough bump and a screeching grind of the gears. The engine died and a door slammed; then the side door was dragged open by a smiling Wendell.

Mason looked at the gun in his hand, glad it was pointed at him instead of Amy.

"Here it is, Mr. Black. Your final stop."

Mason climbed out and a strong ocean breeze rushed at his face as violent rain thrashed against his skin in a flurry. In all his life, he'd never been so damn freezing.

"Dad!"

Desperately relieved to hear her voice, Mason looked

around to where his daughter stood, twenty feet from the edge of the cliff. A thick rope was tied around her leg, and the other end trailed off into the trees. She looked far enough from the edge that she couldn't slip and fall off the cliff. At least that went in their favor.

"Did he hurt you, honey?" He went for her, stopping short as the killer rocketed a punch into his gut. It winded him, sending him to his knees. *He's stronger than he looks.* Mason wanted to hit back—to beat him black and blue—but Wendell was the man with the gun.

"One thing at a time," Wendell told him through gritted teeth. He stepped back, keeping the gun aimed at Mason, and moved toward the trees. Once there, he untied the rope from the trunk, returned, and threw it at Mason. "Tie it around yourself."

What exactly is he planning? "Why?"

Wendell took a quick step forward and pulled back the hammer of the gun. "Just do it."

Mason tied a knot around his waist. With an idea of where this might be heading, he formed a secure loop around his thigh to protect his spine if he fell. "There. You happy? Now let my daughter go."

"All in good time, Mr. Black." He used the gun's barrel to guide Mason to the edge of the cliff, where a strong gust of wind roared at them.

Mason approached and peered over at the drop. It was a hundred feet down, at least, with a rocky bottom. He couldn't help but shiver. *If this is what it takes, then so be it.* But it was then that he noticed it—the one horrific detail that slotted everything into place.

The rope was taut.

"Dad."

Mason turned to his daughter, who trembled from the cold. "Just stay there."

"Don't jump!" she cried, indicating the rope around her leg.

Wendell moved toward Mason, a smug grin crinkling his face. "Here," he said, blocking the space between them, "we have a true test of strength. Tell me, how much do you weigh?"

Mason swallowed hard. "You son of a bitch."

"Happy trails, Mr. Black." He leapt forward and shot out both hands.

As Mason felt the shunt and tumbled backward off the cliff, he heard Amy screaming.

The rope tightened, and he plummeted toward the rocky base of the cliff.

CHAPTER EIGHTY-THREE

Evie's knees struck the ladder with numbing force.

"Shit," she said, wincing as her feet slipped and struggled to get a good grip on the bottom rung. Fighting the pain, she raised her knees, wrapped a sweaty palm around the ladder, and pulled herself up.

It was a bumpy, uncomfortable ride to the cliff's edge. The rain was picking up, and blasts of cold wind rushed at her, but she had to hold on for the sake of her family.

Before they arrived at the edge of the cliff, the engine was cut off and the killer got out, summoning Mason from the side door.

"Here it is, Mr. Black," the killer said. "Your final stop."

Evie lowered herself from the ladder and crept around the side of the RV. From here she could evaluate the situation before making any sudden moves. She could see the gun was pointed at her brother, and her heart raced. Ahead of him, and nearer the cliff's edge, was Amy. She was sobbing but didn't move.

What has he done to you? Evie hated seeing her own niece in danger.

Mason was forced to tie a rope around himself and was then nudged toward the cliff's edge.

No. Evie dropped to a knee and took the knife from her shin strap. She held it how Mason had taught her back at Christmas after presenting her with the gift. Now, she might have to use it, whether she was prepared for that or not.

The killer shoved Mason over the edge of the cliff, and Amy crashed to the ground as the rope dragged her along by her leg. It happened so fast Evie could barely register what was going on. But her instincts kicked in, and there was no need—or time—for caution anymore. She ran forward—not for Wendell, but for the rope.

"Help!" Amy screamed, her voice shrill with panic.

Evie dashed forward, throwing herself to the ground and snagging hold of the rope. She buried her heels into the ground, and the soggy mud rose in a big divot under her feet, slowing them to a stop. "I've got you!"

Wendell stood watching, his expression one of amused surprise. "Not exactly what I hoped for, but I guess this makes things more interesting." He stepped back, holding the gun by his crotch and looking on with excitement.

Evie had to seize control. Using the knife, she sawed feverishly at the rope. The threads came apart, liberating Amy, but Evie was stunned by the sudden increase in weight as she was dragged closer to the cliff face. "Run!" she screamed, demanding Amy get to safety.

Amy hesitated, moved a hand as if to help, then climbed to her feet and sprinted away from the cliff. Within seconds she'd disappeared into the darkness.

"Losing your grip?" Wendell asked, laughing. "I'd love to stay and watch the show, but I have a girl to catch. Adios." He ran after Amy without looking back.

Evie was left alone in the dark, burying her heels as deep as she could into the mud and the rocky ground, but it was no use. She'd merely postponed the inevitable, because Mason was too heavy and she was being hauled closer to the edge. Closer to her brother's death.

She was five yards away.

Three.

Two.

The rocks and mud gave out beneath her and went plummeting off the cliff, while the rope tore at her palms, burning her skin. Exhausted and agonized, Evie yelled at the top of her lungs as the rope finally slipped through her grasp.

CHAPTER EIGHTY-FOUR

A second wind lent Evie a burst of strength, but it wasn't enough.

The rope slipped and burned, and although she managed to plant her feet in hard enough to pull back by a couple of yards, her strength soon waned to nothing.

"Mason," she called. "I can't hold you!" It was near impossible to hear anything through the wind and rain, but she just made out Mason's voice.

"Evie? Where's Amy?"

Evie gritted her teeth and hoisted back. She didn't know how long she could hold on, but it wasn't long. "She escaped... he went after her."

He didn't respond, and Evie grunted as she was dragged closer to the cliff's edge.

"Go," Mason finally yelled, resigned.

Is he crazy? Evie pictured him hanging down there, not as the man he was now, but as the boy she'd played games with on the rug as a kid. The boy who'd taught her to tell time and tie her shoelaces. The brother who'd saved her in every way possible after their parents had died. "I'm not letting you go."

"You have to!"

"No."

"I'm loosening the rope now, Evie. You tried, but it's okay."

Her palms were ablaze as she tried to manage Mason's weight, but it was too much. She suddenly hurtled forward, her chin hitting the dirt as she lost her grip on the rope, and her stomach tore up as she was dragged across the rocks. "Don't you dare fucking untie it," she blurted through a face full of dirt and gravel.

But Mason didn't have to, because the final length of the rope slid from her hand and she stared on in helpless horror as the end flailed around like spaghetti being sucked up, growing shorter and shorter as it raced toward the cliff.

It all happened so fast that she barely heard the rushing patter of footsteps behind her.

Accepting their fate, she closed her eyes and waited for her heart to break.

CHAPTER EIGHTY-FIVE

Mason pulled out a thread of rope, loosening the knot. One more, and he would fall to his death. How else was he supposed to convince Evie to go after Amy?

After everything they'd been through, he cared for only two things: his family's safety, and bringing the Lullaby Killer to justice. If sacrificing himself was the only way to do that, what choice did he have? Besides, it was numbingly cold up here and he was beyond exhausted. Letting go seemed a hell of a lot easier.

He felt a sudden jolt in the rope as the resistance weakened, and he dropped. He fell fast toward the rocks, thoughts of Amy flashing in his mind, and knew Evie must have finally let go. But then there was a brutal jerk, crashing him into the jagged cliff face and tearing his arm to shreds.

"Don't let go!" boomed a familiar voice from above. A man's voice.

"Bill?" Mason strained to look up.

"Whatever you do, just don't let go. We're going to pull you up, buddy."

We? As Mason was hoisted up the cliff, he wondered who the hell would be there to thank. He prayed it wasn't Evie, and that she'd gone after Wendell.

When he got to the top, rocks grazing his arms and legs while the cold wind blasted at his back, Bill and Evie pulled him to his feet. Evie was caked in mud, holding her arms in pain. It must have taken everything she had to hold him for that long. But his gratitude could wait.

"Where did Amy go?" Mason demanded, clambering to his feet and moving away from the cliff.

"The trees," Evie said, pointing a finger. "Let's go."

"No." Mason stopped her. "You stay here. Bill, give me your gun."

"We'll both be in a lot of trouble if you—"

"Give me the damn gun!"

Bill drew it from his hip and handed it over, not saying another word.

"You got a car?" Mason stared into the dark woods.

"Yeah."

"Good. Take Evie. I need to finish this." He turned, and without another word, he started off along the sodden ground, his jog speeding into a run. Putting the last of his depleted energy into chasing the infamous Lullaby Killer for the final time, Mason sprinted off into the trees.

CHAPTER EIGHTY-SIX

Mason had never run so fast in his life. As branches and thick bushes tried to slow him down, clawing at his shredded arm, he pummeled through them with immeasurable force.

Wendell was ahead of him, just close enough to see in the darkness of the murky woods. He, too, was moving at great speed. Only he wasn't running away from Mason. He was plowing after Amy in what was a terrifying pursuit.

Mason slowed down, fatigue weighing down his feet. "Stop right there!" he yelled, clutching the gun tight. He stepped over a fallen branch and aimed the gun. It was now or never—a wild shot, or lose the killer and Amy.

Holding his breath, then letting it out, he coiled his finger around the trigger and squeezed. The gunshot echoed through the trees, startling birds and making them scatter.

Wendell stopped dead in his tracks, raising his hands.

Amy fell into the dirt not far beyond.

"Don't move, asshole." Mason stepped forward. Amy came into view. She was on the ground, skin scraped and cut after her escape from the Lullaby Killer.

"Dad," she whined. "Stop him. Please stop him."

"Yeah, Dad." Wendell stepped closer, his evil grin illuminated in the moonlight. "Stop me." It was an obvious taunt, and far too tempting.

Mason gripped the gun harder, trembling in the cold and eager to make a move. He stepped over a pile of dead leaves and looked around.

You have no idea how much I want to kill you.

"Shoot him, Dad!" Amy cried.

"He won't, little girl. We don't know why, but he won't." Wendell sidestepped, inclining his head a little to examine Mason's expression. "Is it because of his moral code? Is that it? Or is it because his daughter is watching?"

"She's seen worse things than you," Mason spat through clenched teeth.

"I don't doubt it. But I wager she's never seen anything as *interesting* as me. Ain't that right?" Wendell wouldn't keep still, cowering only slightly at the sight of the gun. "I mean, look at this. It took you years to catch me, and now you finally have, you can't even bring yourself to stop me."

"Don't flatter yourself." There was something wrong. Mason could feel it. Was the killer really that confident he wouldn't shoot? *Would* he shoot? The logical thing to do would be to bring him in for arrest. But there was something telling him he couldn't. Something saying it would be his worst move. All the same, he could easily bluff it. "Do you know what they do to child killers in prison?"

"Oh, come on. You know as well as I do I'm not ever heading that way. Here you are, deciding whether to shoot me. But, we both know—" Wendell came closer and lowered his hands. "—that doing so would make you as bad as me. You're not a killer, are you, Mr. Black?"

Mason knew his options. They were limited, but at least he *had* options. He glanced at Amy, who was hurt and frightened. The idea that anyone would make his daughter feel that way only enraged him with bloodlust. He looked back at Wendell, the Lullaby Killer who'd caused him so much trouble for all these years.

"No," he said. "I'm far worse."

CHAPTER EIGHTY-SEVEN

Evie was in Bill's car when she saw them. However, she felt both thrilled and disappointed at the same time. Seeing Mason was a relief, and laying eyes on Amy meant she could relax a little. *But where the hell is Wendell?*

Bill was first out the car, rushing straight to Mason while Evie ran to her niece, crouching to hold her close. "Are you okay? I'm so sorry."

Amy hugged her back, sobbing into her shoulder as the cruel rain continued to fall.

"Evie." Mason looked down and placed a hand on Amy's back. "Can you take her to the car for me? I need to talk to Bill."

"What? Where's Wendell?"

Mason shook his head and swallowed. "He got away."

While he and Bill talked among themselves, Evie carried a sobbing Amy to the car and sat cradling her to warm her up. The police and an ambulance were on their way, so they could give their statements and have their injuries taken care of.

But Evie couldn't take her eyes off her brother.

What aren't you telling me?

Mason was talking as Bill ran his fingers through his hair, looking as stressed as ever. They were obviously sharing a secret, and Evie wanted in. Frustrated, she would just have to wait.

Mason returned to the car, stroking Amy's hair.

"Got away, huh?" Evie whispered, sighing.

"Yes."

"Listen, you don't have to tell me everything. You *never* have to say more than you feel comfortable with. But don't ever lie to me. Understood?" Evie felt horrible for putting it so bluntly. Was she being paranoid? Everything they'd been through had certainly taught her to be cautious, if nothing else.

Mason lowered his head. "I'm not lying. In fact, I've decided to drop the case."

"Drop it?" *This is definitely not like him.* "What the hell do you mean?"

"I have Amy back, although worse for wear. The only reason this happened is because I was getting too deep into things. I've spoken to Bill, and he'll continue the investigation without me."

"We'll want the official statement," Bill said from the driver's side.

"Can we swing by in the morning?" Mason hoisted

Amy from the car and carried her to the approaching ambulance.

"I don't see why not."

Evie climbed out and went with Mason, resigning to his terrible idea of giving up. Something was definitely off, whether he was willing to admit it or not. Maybe it was best if she never found out.

For now, however, she had a niece to take care of and a brother to support. In spite of his poor choice, Mason would still need her. And who was she to refuse?

CHAPTER EIGHTY-EIGHT

Mason had no sooner got his daughter back than he had to hand her away again.

The doctors had seen to her cuts and near-broken finger, and she'd taken it like a champ. No whining, as might be expected from a thirteen-year-old. No moaning, or any signs of posttraumatic stress. In fact, she showed nothing but gratitude that she'd made it out of there alive.

It was more than Evie could have handled—she'd cringed at her own scrapes and gone home to rest after making sure everyone was okay.

Finally, it was just Mason and Amy, the loving father-daughter duo.

"You ready to go?" he asked, picking her up as if she was still five.

Amy nodded and wrapped her arms around him as he carried her out to the Mustang.

Mason messed with the keys. His hands were shaking like crazy, but he had no idea why. *Probably just fatigue,* he thought, and closed his fist tight and opened it again, easing the tension. *Better*. He started the engine, and the headlights lit up the dark.

"You're never coming home, are you?" Amy asked as he pulled out of the hospital parking lot. It seemed as if she knew the answer but wanted to hear it from his own lips.

"I don't think so."

They soon arrived at the house, and Mason tried not to think about the divorce papers. Instead, he thought only about what to do next. Hunting down Marvin Wendell was sure as hell not on his list of priorities, but private investigating might still be an option.

Mason climbed out of the car and opened the door for Amy. He took her hand and helped her out of the car, then walked her toward the house.

"Wait." Amy stopped, halfway up the driveway.

"What is it?"

"I want to live with you."

Mason would have loved it, too, but it simply wasn't possible. He kneeled, brushed the stray strands of hair over her ear, and looked her in the eye. "I don't have anywhere to live yet, sweetheart. I'm still living with Bill."

"What about when you're ready?"

"Maybe." *It depends what the court decides*, he thought but didn't say.

Just then, the front door of the house sprang open and Sandra came running out. She was barefoot but didn't care and almost knocked Amy off her feet as she grabbed her and encased her in a hug.

"I'm so sorry I let you go," Sandra said, planting firm kisses on her cheek. She looked at Mason, grabbed his T-shirt, and pulled him close, holding him, too. "I'm so sorry."

Mason wasn't sure if she was repeating her apology to Amy, or offering a new one to him. Whoever it was for, he hugged her back, holding her close and knowing this was the last time he would ever see such affection from his wife.

Over her shoulder, he saw Joshua walking down the drive. He had his head down, but his eyes were up. When he stopped, he lowered his gaze to his feet. "I just wanted to say—"

"Shut up," Mason barked. "You're not a part of this." God knew he wanted to hit Joshua. For taking his wife. For trying to take his daughter. And for ever letting Amy get in harm's way in the first place.

"You know what?" Sandra whispered in Mason's ear, still clutching him. "Maybe we should rethink a few things."

Mason felt it like a sucker punch. He knew it was probably just the elation of the moment that made her say it, but how was he supposed to respond? His initial reaction was to smile, to say *Great!* and *Everything will be okay*. But in spite of his own mistakes throughout their marriage, could he ever really accept the way she'd handled it?

As difficult as it was, he said nothing, rubbing his

tired eyes and breaking free of the embrace. "I'd better head home."

"We'll talk tomorrow," Sandra told him, nodding.

"Sure." Mason kissed his daughter on the cheek and mussed her hair. "See you soon." He went back to his car, started the engine, and pulled out of the drive. In the rearview mirror he saw his wife and daughter standing and waving him off. Joshua skulked in the background.

Go get some rest, he could imagine Evie saying. Mason wanted to take that advice, and he certainly would. But there was somewhere else he had to go first. It was something he'd started earlier that night but hadn't quite finished.

Now that he was alone, he could finally do it.

CHAPTER EIGHTY-NINE

"I hate to say it, Mason, but I'm disappointed in you." Captain Cox pushed back from the table and went to the door, holding it open for him to leave.

After a few hours' sleep, he'd returned to give the entirety of his statement and his reasons for terminating his pursuit of Marvin Wendell. "I'm sorry I couldn't be more help," he said, shooting a look at Bill, who stood clutching a clipboard.

The three of them left the room together. The captain headed toward her office, while Bill showed Mason to the coffee machine. It felt like a cliché spot for a private discussion, but they had to talk while they had the chance.

"Where were you this morning?" Bill asked, looking skeptical.

"Cleaning up after you. The cameras needed wiping, you know." Mason just wished the man would be more careful. If they were going to pull this off, they had to work as a team. Any half-hearted efforts could end them.

"Okay." Bill glanced around, dug into his pocket for the key, and slid it into Mason's hand. "Make sure nobody sees you. I'll have to catch up later."

"When?"

"I'm off duty at five, so hang in there."

Mason stuffed the key into his pocket and walked toward the side exit. The front of the police station was swarming with press, who had somehow gotten wind of the situation and made it public. That was bad for everyone.

In the alleyway beside the building, Evie stood gazing at the beautiful morning sky. Although she'd begged for an explanation from Mason, he had nothing more to offer her. The best he could do was assure her the killer would move on from San Francisco.

"Get in," he said, opening the car door.

He drove her back to her apartment and stopped outside in peaceful silence.

"Will you be all right?" she asked.

"I'll live." Mason wondered how he was going to convince her that he'd simply shied away from hunting Wendell. After all the judgment he'd received from Captain Cox, the last thing he wanted was Evie to be disappointed with him. "I'm looking at apartments tomorrow."

"Oh? Not getting back with Sandra, then?" she said, a tone of sadness in her voice.

"I doubt it. There are other things for me out there, you know?"

"Yeah." Evie sat back in the seat, the half-open door letting the cool winter air in. "That's great about the apartment though. But how will you pay for it?"

Mason had asked himself the same thing, and now the answer seemed clearer than ever. "I think it's time to reopen the office. I can take on other cases, ones I don't associate with my time on the police force."

Evie smiled and kissed him on the cheek. "It's what you're good at." She climbed out of the car, closed the door, and headed into her apartment building, looking over her shoulder and giving a little wave.

Mason was looking forward to the life he'd just described. It would be dangerous, sure, yet he would miss it if it weren't there.

But there was still one thing left to finish before he could move on, something he couldn't possibly have told Evie or the captain.

Checking the key was still tucked away in his pocket, he looked around to make sure he wasn't followed, then drove to where he needed to be.

CHAPTER NINETY

The shipping container sat at the back of the lot, where it was quiet and out of the way—no wonder Bill had chosen it. Mason checked his surroundings before sliding the key into the heavy-duty padlock and opening it up. It was dark inside, but Mason had to lock the door from the inside before he could use the internal lamp.

Clunk.

The room lit up, and Mason turned to face the back, where an orange glow illuminated Marvin Wendell. The man was a mess: naked, chained up tight, and silenced by a homemade ball gag Bill had made with a snooker ball and a belt. It looked painful as hell, but it was no less than he deserved.

"Morning, asshole." Mason stepped forward and removed his jacket, placing it on the upturned crates. "Bill wanted me to wait until he got here, but I don't see why we can't just get started."

Wendell struggled to break free of his chains, but nothing happened.

Mason walked slowly to the gurney, admiring the detail Bill had gone to. He understood the man's pain, too—Wendell had killed Bill and Christine's son. That was enough to make anybody crazy for revenge.

"You know, you made a big mistake by hurting my daughter." Mason pulled the dust sheet off the tray, revealing a pile of rusted surgical tools.

Crying and screaming behind the gag, Wendell thrashed against the chains.

Mason picked up the first tool and held it up to the light. It looked like a bottle opener, a kind of blade with clamps. *We'll start with this.* "Now, hold still. You wouldn't want me to miss."

When Mason was done, he and Bill would burn the body and try to pass it off as an unsolved murder. It may not be the official closure of the case—they may not even get away with it—but it would bring the Lullaby Killer to the horrific end he deserved while administering justice to all the families he'd destroyed.

Grinding his teeth, Mason got to work on punishing Wendell, blissfully unaware he'd been followed to the site.

If only he knew he'd just opened a whole new can of worms.

ALSO BY

ADAM NICHOLLS

MASQUERADE

Mason Black #2 is now available on Amazon.

AFTERWORD

Let me start by saying a huge thank you for making it through to the end. It means so much to me that you found this book worth your time, and that's the kind of thing that keeps me writing.

Some of you are new to my work, but those who aren't will have recognized this story. *Missing* was originally published as *Hush* back in 2016 and was (somehow) even more violent. Some of the other changes to this title have been subtle, while some serious components to the story have been completely realigned. You're probably asking yourself why such significant events have been altered, and the answer is this: it's what the market demands.

If you're on my mailing list, you'll know that I'm currently going through a major relaunch for some of my older books. Some are getting new titles, and all of them are having their covers and blurbs redone. Furthermore, they're all being translated to US English (as opposed to the original UK English). This is because more of my readership comes from the United States, and in the interest of keeping a roof over my head, I need to cater to the good folks of America.

So, what's next? Well, after this trilogy is published I'll be working on brand-new stories of mystery and suspense, which I simply can't wait to get to you. My head is buzzing with ideas, and I've never been so excited to get them down on paper.

If you're still with me, let me thank you again for taking the time to read this book. I sincerely hope you found the stories worth your time, and perhaps even subscribe to my mailing list or like my Facebook page to keep in touch. I'm always eager to talk with fans.

After all, you're who I write for.

My best,
Adam Nicholls

ABOUT THE AUTHOR

Adam Nicholls has been creating stories since before he could legally drink. Inspired by the works of Stephen King, Karin Slaughter and Gillian Flynn, Adam starts writing each new book by asking himself how best to shock his readers.

In his non-writing life, Adam is a bibliophile and avid collector of anything made from paper (utility bills included). He loves hot showers, good wine and the sound of rain hitting the window. Whenever possible, he likes to get out and see the world, visiting one European city at a time in search of inspiration for his next great novel.

Get in touch:
www.adamnichollsauthor.com
contact@adamnichollsauthor.com

Printed in Poland
by Amazon Fulfillment
Poland Sp. z o.o., Wrocław